The Crook of Marsden Manor

by G. H. Teed

First published as No. 224 (New Series),
—Sexton Blake Library. January 1930.

THE **CROOK** OF **MARSDEN MANOR**

In this thrilling crime story SEXTON BLAKE is working against the notorious international adventurer, George Marsden Plummer—and an astounding plot is brought to light.

Stillwoods Edition, 2019

Stillwoods.Blogspot.Ca

Catlogue Information

Title: The Crook of Marsden Manor

Author: G. H. Teed (1886-1938)

First Published: Sexton Blake Library. January 1930, No. 224 (New Series).

This Edition by: Stillwoods, 2019

Blog: Stillwoods.Blogspot.Ca

Storefront: http://www.lulu.com/spotlight/lulubook22

Author's Blog: http://ghteed.blogspot.com/

ISBN Canada: 978-1-988304-66-3

Sexton Blake Library

The Leading Detective-Story Magazine

In this thrilling crime story SEXTON BLAKE is working against the notorious international adventurer, George Marsden Plummer—and an astounding plot is brought to light.

'George Marsden Plummer — master crook and international adventurer! This is the dynamic influence behind the colossal swindles that are amazing London and Paris. The action of this sensational novel moves swiftly between the two capitals. Robbery and murder lead to Sexton Blake's entry upon a case that is enthralling in its vivid description of Apache villainy and the scheming of a super crook.'

G. H. Teed was born in New Brunswick, Canada and was educated at McGill University, Montreal, Quebec. He went on to travel the world supporting himself by writing detective thrillers published in magazines in London, U.K.

This is a reproduction of one of those thrillers which are so hard to find today.

Doug Frizzle, February, 2019.

Chapter 1.   Machines of Mystery.

IN both the home and export bicycle markets, as well as among the light steel trades generally, there could be no doubt about the instantaneous success of the Marsden bicycle. Before it had been on the market three months it had set a record in England and France that was the envy of every manufacturer who turned out a machine of its class; and it was authoritatively reported by the vast army of overseas agents among the Dominions and Colonies that the new Marsden was cutting in seriously.

It had been launched with a wide fanfare of advertising. Every newspaper in the kingdom had carried full-page announcements on the same day containing an attractive picture of a young man and a young woman bowling gaily along a lovely country road bounded by fields, in the midst of which could be seen a delightful little stream.

The machines they were riding were, of course, the soon-to-be-famous Marsdens; and then followed a cleverly written account of the great factory at Slough, in Bucks, where these ultra-perfect machines were turned out at so many hundreds every day. The article had been composed by a well-known cyclist, whose name was one to conjure with in the cycling world and among the thousands of club riders throughout the country.

And if that was not enough, there was the positive guarantee that the Marsden was to be sold at the flat price of £4 each for the gentlemen's model and £4 5s. for the super ladies' model, as against £4 15s. 6d. and £4 19s. 6d. respectively, charged by other manufacturers for exactly the same machine.

Great stress was laid on this comparison in prices, and the guarantee which was attached to each bicycle contained a clause stating that the manufacturers would pay the sum of £1.000 in cash to any person, be he a rival manufacturer or not, who could prove that any and every statement made in connection with the Marsden was not true to the last detail.

Every journal devoted to cycling and motor-cycling, every trade paper connected in any way with engineering or the light steel trades, all the overseas editions of the big London dailies—every possible advertising medium, indeed, had been employed to launch the great boom of the Marsden's, and secret observers from other factories who went to Slough could only report to their principals that the Marsden factory was running at full blast.

Among the millions of persons who scanned their papers each

morning, and who could not escape the blatant announcement of the Marsden bicycle, was Mr. Sexton Blake, the famous detective of Baker Street, London. His interest in the advertisement was purely perfunctory, and after a brief glance at the particulars, he turned the page, commenting inwardly as he did so: "Another new bicycle on the market, and, apparently, plenty of money behind it. It seems as if industry is looking up somewhat."

But his young assistant, Tinker, gave the announcement a more detailed study, for it was a subject in which he was interested. Yet the result was no more than for the lad to wonder how this new machine could be turned out at so much less than other standard bicycles if the material employed were of as high a quality. And certainly neither anticipated for a single moment that, some three months after the first advertisements appeared, Blake's services were to be sought in connection with a matter connected with this same thing.

It was on a crisp, sunny morning, when Blake and the lad were engaged on the routine work of going through the morning mail, that a card was brought in by Mrs. Bardell. The piece of pasteboard bore the name of

Mr. PETER J. MENDLEY,

and the address showed that he came from Birmingham. Then in the lower left-hand corner was:

"Messrs. Mendley, Ltd.,

Cycle Manufacturers."

The name was not unknown to Blake, for the Mendley bicycle was one of the best-known machines in England, or, indeed, throughout the world. For years their advertisements had been familiar to him—the picture of a man riding a Mendley, and, accompanying it, the slogan: "Ride as you Pay—Pay as you Ride."

He laid the card on his desk and told Mrs. Bardell to show the visitor in. A few moments later a stocky man of pleasant countenance, with grey hair, grey moustache, and wearing a grey suit, entered. His step was brisk, his eyes clear and direct in their regard, his hand clasp firm, but not forced, his whole manner one of a man who knows the value of time and values it accordingly.

Blake shook hands and drew a chair forward. In the swift, measuring glance which could tell him so much, he knew that this visitor was a pipe man, and would refuse cigars or cigarettes; so, taking up his own pipe, he pushed across the miniature cask in which he kept his own choice mixture.

With a quick smile that showed two even rows of strong white teeth, his visitor took out a dark, polished briar and helped himself to a wad of mixture that proved the exact quantity needed to pack the bowl to the brim. When it was alight he leaned back, and blew an appreciative sniff after the cloud of smoke he had sent ceiling-wards.

"Good stuff, Mr. Blake, good stuff! Must get you to tell me the secret. But I didn't come to waste your time discussing tobacco. Your time is valuable; so is mine. How long can you spare me?"

"How long do you need, Mr. Mendley?"

"About twenty minutes if you are not interested; half an hour or so if you accept the business I am going to offer you."

"Fire away; I am listening. If you don't interest me I shall soon tell you."

"That's the way I want it. Ever hear of the Mendley bicycle?"

"Of course. I have seen the advertisements for years past, and, if I remember rightly, I rode one many years ago. I fancy this young man, my assistant, has ridden one also."

"If you rode one it would be about the time I first joined my father in the firm. But that gives us a starter. I am the head of the firm now."

"So I gathered from your card."

The manufacturer nodded.

"For years past there hasn't been a more popular or better-selling bicycle than the Mendley. It isn't only in the home market that we have scooped the cream of the business, but in the export markets as well. I won't bore you with figures now, because they are not necessary for my purpose, but it will be enough to say that we exported more than half a million bicycles last year, and the figures should have been exceeded this year; but they won't be, and that is what has brought me to you. More than fifty thousand machines to India alone; thirty odd thousand to West Africa, more than a hundred thousand to South Africa and Australia, seventy-five thousand to New Zealand, fifty thousand to Canada, and so on and so on. Good business, as you will realise, and one that is worth keeping. Nor is it because of any falling off in the quality of the Mendley that our figures are down. The quality is as good to-day, if not even a wee bit better than ever before. And it isn't the industrial depression you hear so much about."

"My own information tells me that the situation is greatly improved," murmured Blake.

"And so it is. Now then, Mr. Blake; you are a business man as well as a detective. I took the trouble to learn something about you before I came to seek your aid. My friend, Sir George Barron, told me about the concession in the Philippines which you secured for his syndicate —but I'll spare your blushes."

Blake smiled faintly, but said nothing.

"I have asked you about the Mendley," went on the visitor; "and now I want to ask you if you know anything about a new bicycle that has been on the market a matter of three months or so—the Marsden, it is called."

"I recall reading the newspaper advertisements of a machine of that name some little time ago, but I am afraid my knowledge of it begins and ends there. Perhaps Tinker—"

He turned to the lad, who was sitting at his desk in the corner, listening.

"What about it, young 'un?"

"I've seen the machine, guv'nor; it's a nice-looking bit of work, from the look of it, but I haven't ridden one yet."

Peter Mendley gave Tinker a quick searching look; then he nodded.

"Your assistant is right, Mr. Blake. It is a nice looking bit of work, and it is a good bit of work as well. Even though it is manufactured by a rival, and is the chief cause of my coming to you this morning I cannot honostly detract from the quality of the machine."

"But I don't quite follow you, Mr. Mendley."

"Let me explain. Until those advertisements appeared some three months ago the Marsden bicycle was unheard of. It was a coup. I don't deny that. The people behind the thing secured their factory, installed their assembling machinery and other machines, got all their contracts for parts fixed both in this country, and on the Continent, and had fifty thousand finished machines ready to spring on the Home market before a whisper leaked out. That was clever; it showed a first-class directing brain behind it all."

"It would seem so."

"Well, you can imagine that when I read the first advertisements I lost no time in looking into the business. It was a thing that struck at the very root of my own manufacture, and I wanted to find out just how strong these now rivals were. Also there was the guarantee which they made such a strong point of in their announcements. You may not recall the price fixed for the Marsden, but it was four pounds for a man's machine, and four pounds five shillings for a woman's machine. That compared with four pounds fifteen shillings and sixpence and four pounds nineteen shillings and six-pence respectively for the same class machines turned out by me and other factories. And they made an offer of one thousand pounds to anyone, even another manufacturer, if it could be proved that any single part was inferior to the same part in any other standard make sold at the last prices I have named."

"I do remember that."

"The first thing I did was to buy a dozen Marsden bicycles in the open retail market. I fixed it so it could not be known whom they were for. Then I had my engineers take those machines and strip them to the bare frame. There wasn't a bearing, there wasn't a cog, there wasn't a square inch of metal that my men didn't put through every possible known test. And they stood up to it."

"Would it be possible that this new firm was willing to lose money on, say, the first hundred thousand machines for the sake of getting established? I have known cigarette manufacturers to put out a most excellent cigarette at a low price until they secured a number of consumers, and then to lower the quality of the tobacco gradually until they got back far more than they lost in the first place."

"That also occurred to me. So I played a waiting game. I have bought no fewer than seventy-five Marsden bicycles during the past three months, and each one has been subjected to the same stringent tests. I have secured them from every part of England, and have even had them bought and shipped to me from France, Germany and other places abroad. But not in one single case have we found an inferior bit of work. And yet I know it can't be done at the figure at which they are being sold. Even supposing the manufacturers of the Marsden had fixed contracts for different parts at a price considerably below that at which I and other manufacturers are buying it would not account for the wide difference in price. In the one model there is a difference of no less than fifteen shillings and sixpence, and in the other a difference of fourteen shillings and sixpence. I tell you, it can't be done. Mr. Blake—not and show a profit. Nor is that all. Take the question of their overhead charges, their cost of production. My work-people are among the best paid in the country. They are also on a profit sharing basis, and are as satisfied as can be. And yet the Marsden factory pays, on an average, eight shillings per week per head more than the average pay of my hands, including their bonuses and share of profits. To come down to actual figures I calculate that the Marsden is being marketed at a gross profit of not more than four shillings per machine, and if you take the overhead cost of each machine out of that you will find a net loss on each machine of about ninepence. That is what convinces me after three months that there must be a 'nigger in the woodpile' somewhere. And I can tell you that if I don't find it pretty soon this new bicycle is going to play Old Harry with my export trade."

"But what do you expect me to do, Mr. Mendley?"

"I will tell you. I have had three of my most trusted men in employ at the Marsden factory at different times. They have kept their eyes and ears open, but have discovered nothing. If there is any monkey business coming on it is beyond the scope of men of that sort. On the face of it the whole business is open enough and just a successful new venture from the point of view of sales. But keep in mind what I said about profits. No company, unless it were controlled by lunatics, would continue to sell at a loss; and I know they can't be making a profit. If I don't learn that secret it means I shall have to make complete reorganisation of my plant and put on the market a new machine under the name of Mendley that will be inferior in quality to the present one that I am selling under that name. I hate to do such a thing, for the word Mendley has always stood for first quality. But I've got to meet competition or close my factory. Therefore I am determined to make one more effort to discover how the trick is being turned. It may seem a far cry from the detection of criminals, but you are the sort of professional investigator to take on the job if you will be persuaded to do so. There is my proposition, Mr. Blake. Will you accept the commission? You can name your own fee, and I won't look at your expense account."

Sexton Blake rubbed his chin thoughtfully. What Mendley had just said was quite true—there seemed little connection between an investigation to determine how one manufacturer of bicycles was clever enough to put out a complete machine of first grade at a price considerably lower than practically the same bicycle marketed by a man who had been at the game all his life, and confessed that he was working on a close margin of profit.

At the same time the investigation of an industrial question of this nature was a little outside the scope of Blake's regular work. It was true that as his visitor had mentioned, he had undertaken a mission to the Philippine Islands on behalf of a rich London financial syndicate, and had returned with a rich concession tucked in his pocket.

And at one time and another he had probed industrial questions in the Midlands and the North. But bicycles! To try and discover why one man was selling a machine a few shillings cheaper than another! He glanced whimsically at his visitor.

"You say you have already had three of your most trusted men in the Marsden factory at Slough."

"Yes, but they were mechanics, intelligent, capable men, it is true, but not the sort to discover what might be going on underneath."

"You spoke of contracts for different parts—just what did you mean, Mr. Mendley?"

"Some factories manufacture their own parts completely and assemble their machines on the spot; others manufacture only certain parts, say the frame, and contract either in this country or abroad for the other parts; and, lastly, some factories contract with different manufacturers for every part, only using their premises for assembling. Thus a machine may be wholly of British make or may be of English and foreign parts combined, or, still again altogether of foreign parts assembled in this country."

"I see. How would you classify the Mendley?"

"In the second class. I manufacture my own frames of the finest grade of chrome steel, also my handle-bars, sprockets and other plated parts. The rest I secure on contract through other makers."

"All British?"

"Not altogether; a few parts I import from France."

"And the Marsden?"

"As far as I can discover it is made up entirely of parts manufactured by other people. The factory at Slough is only used for assembling."

"Are the contracts placed in this country?"

"There seems no definite arrangement about that. For instance one of the men I had at Slough told me the frames that were delivered while he was there came from a maker in Sheffield; another told me that during his period in the factory the frames came from the Continent."

"But the two would have to be of the same testing standard?"

"Oh. yes—strictly to specification."

Blake filled his pipe again and pondered the matter. There was one matter of considerable importance in hand at the moment, but for a reason he could scarcely explain he had a feeling he would like to look into this matter which Mendley had laid before him. It was so different from the usual run of things that came his way.

At last he turned his gaze towards the manufacturer.

"All right, Mr. Mendley," he said crisply. "I'll take it on, but I do not promise to tell you why one bicycle should sell at a price considerably lower than another of the same class. I want a few particulars to go on with. Come here, Tinker, and take down what Mr. Mendley says."

They set to work then, and during the next hour or so, while Blake probed and analysed the question of bicycles, their manufacture and marketing, it did not cross his mind that what appeared to be an orthodox business investigation, was going to link up with one of the biggest criminal coups that had been pulled off for many years past; nor could he guess that therein was to be found the answer to the riddle of price differences which was threatening to destroy the home and export business of the Mendley Cycle Co., Ltd.

CHAPTER 2.   Tinker's New Job.

WHETHER Peter J. Mendiey was right or wrong in suspecting that some ramp lay behind the activities of the Marsden Cycle Co., there could be not the slightest question that, outwardly, at least, the business at Slough was perfectly genuine.

The plant was housed in one of those big, well-lighted buildings which have spread over a large area at Slough since the war—vast sheds which carry all their machinery on the ground floor, and which are provided with their own railway sidings.

Its front faced the main Great Western line that runs from Paddington to the West Country, and above the great, double-swing doors was the sign:

MARSDEN CYCLES.

Most of the employees dwelt in little cottages close at hand, although a few still came from London each morning or districts in the vicinity, waiting until the new cottages which the company was building should be ready for occupancy.

Nor was Peter J. Mendley's spy mistaken when he said the Marsden employees were well content with their lot. It was true that their pay averaged some eight shillings a week more than other factories of the same description were paying; their cottages were modern, well-built little houses each having its own bath-room; there was a sports club with extensive grounds; a large gymnasium with swimming tank attached; tennis courts, and, indeed, every possible amenity for social intercourse and recreation which the employer of old would have scorned as entirely unnecessary, but which the modern industrialist recognises as a very profitable investment in that he receives dividends in content and increased efficiency which nothing else can supply.

Close to the private railway siding which served the factory were the receiving and shipping sheds. In the former were stored the bicycle frames and various other parts which would be assembled in the factory, or, as Mendley had told Sexton Blake, the Marsden people were assemblers only, not manufacturing a single part that went to the making of the machine which bore their name.

On the eastern side of the building, also close to the railway siding, were the general offices of the company, with, at the back of these, the private bureau of the president and general manager, Mr. Gerald Marsden—so one found stated on the business paper of the firm.

It has taken many businesses a long time to discover the truth of the well-worn statement that "It pays to advertise"; but the Marsden Cycle Co. was handicapped by no such lack of belief. Its advertising manager was a young man who had had his training first in the advertising department of one of the great papers of Fleet Street, had transferred to a firm of advertising specialists, where he had successfully conducted nation-wide campaigns, and was exactly ripe for the launching of a new product like the Marsden Cycle when that firm broke into the market.

The success of his efforts began to show almost as soon as the announcements appeared in the Press. And if anyone had doubted the magnitude of the results that followed, and were continuing to grow with the rapidity of a snowball rolling downhill, he need but glance at the dozen or so big sales books which hold contracts from every section of the British Isles and almost every part of the globe.

It was only natural that, despite the huge total of unemployed in the country, the Marsden Cycle Co. should not find it an easy matter to fill the ranks of employees. The work of assembling was a specialised job that was distributed scientifically—that is to say, the bare frame of the machine was taken in hand at one end of the factory, and passed along by wide belts between double ranks of men until it emerged at the other end of the factory a completed model.

From the moment the frames came out of the ovens where the red enamel that was the colour adopted by the Marsden people was baked on, each man had one job and one job only to perform. In this case it would be the fitting of the wheels, in that, the sprockets, in another the chains, still again the adjustment of the ball bearings, and so and so on. Efficiency with speed—that was the watchword of the factory.

It wasn't long before word spread throughout the country of the excellent wages and ideal conditions of work at the Slough factory. Men began to steal away from other work of the same nature in order to apply to the Marsden company for work. Every man, if he knew his job, was accepted without question, for orders were coming in so fast that the demand could not be coped with.

There was no difficulty, therefore, when, on a certain day in early autumn, a young workman appeared at the staff window and asked for a chance to sign on. The employment director—a man who was a specialist in industrial psychology—studied the young man carefully for a few minutes, then asked abruptly:

"You are qualified for this sort of work?"

"Yes, sir."

"What particular branch?"

"I understand the work here is assembling, sir; I have had experience in the fitting of bearings."

"Where have you been working?"

"At a private garage."

"London or the provinces?"

"London, sir— just off Baker Street."

"You have references?"

"Yes, sir; will you look at them, please," As he spoke, the youthful applicant drew out a somewhat soiled envelope from which he took a couple of folded papers. One of these stated that "Charles Turner" was a qualified motor mechanic and had passed the full test demanded by the Western Garage, of Baker Street, London; the second informed whom it might concern that Charles Turner had passed a special test in the fittings and bearings, and was thoroughly competent to fill such a position in connection with either motor-cycles or pedal bicycles.

The man behind the window handed the papers back and made a gesture towards a stiff wooden chair that stood against the wall just behind the applicant.

"Sit down and wait," he said curtly.

Then, as the young man obeyed, he walked to his desk, sat down, drew the receiver towards him, and gave the number of the Western Garage, which he had learned from the heading of the papers he had been examining. It was plain that he was not one to accept written testimonials without checking them up.

The applicant could hear all that passed at his end of the telephone. But he wasn't worrying. Everything said in the two certificates was quite true, with one exception—his baptismal name wasn't "Charles Turner," any more than any other baptismal name. Yet, as Tinker, he was probably better known than any other lad in the whole British Empire. On the other hand, there is no law in England against a person taking any name which pleases his fancy, so, for the time being, "Charles Turner" was his monniker.

As for his qualifications as a mechanic, the statements were quite in order. Not only did he possess the much coveted certificate issued to approved men by the Rolls-Royce Company—and Blake's big Rolls, the Grey Panther was, to Tinker, as a child to its mother—but it and his own motor-cycle were kept at the Western Garage, just back of Blake's house in Baker Street, and there wasn't any test in that place that Tinker hadn't passed. Furthermore, it was quite true that he had specialised in bearings, both ball and cone, so when he had asked for the two documents they had been forthcoming at once.

The staff man hung up the receiver, and his manner was a little less curt as he once more surveyed the young man.

"You can sign on," he announced "When can you begin?"

"At once."

"Well, you had better leave it until the afternoon. Come here a few minutes before twelve, and you can meet the foreman of your department. In the meantime, you will have a chance to look up lodgings. Better go to the place where most of our unmarried men stay—the gatekeeper will show you. I'll have your card ready, and you receive the standard rate of wages. The foreman will explain everything and fix you up in your place. That's all!"

Tinker tlmnked him and made his way out. The gate-keeper directed him to the big red-brick building where he would find lodgings, and then, when he had picked up the bag he had left at the station, he walked round to the place. He was given a cubicle-room, which was scrupulously clean, with its own basin and running tap in one corner. The bed was a good one, and the lad could not help but reflect that the Marsden people certainly took care to look after their workpeople.

From the lodging-house he went to the post-ofiice, where he put through a call to Sexton Blake. When he was through, he informed Blake, that he had secured a place and gave him the address of his lodgings. Then he rang off and, having at least a couple of hours on his hands before he would have to report once more, he strolled towards the private railway siding that served the Marsden factory.

A number of goods trucks were standing on the metals, and, from the one nearest the open door of the receiving warehouse, men were wheeling in hand-trucks loaded with wooden crates containing what the lad took to be steel bicycle frames. No one interfered with him, so he drew closer until he could count the number of frames in each crate—six he made it.

Through the open door of the warehouse he could see a long vista of piles and piles of similar crates. He figured there must be several thousand frames already stored there waiting to be enamelled and sent to the baking ovens; and still they poured in. This, alone, was proof sufficient that the business of the firm was genuine enough.

When he had satisfied himself on that point, he made his way past the long side of the factory, and round the end of the goods trucks. until he came to the other door where the finished product was being loaded into empty trucks. These machines, like the frames, were packed in wooden crates, the additional protection of "excelsior" and strong brown paper being employed over the enamelled and plated parts.

After a little strategy, Tinker managed to get close to the edge of the loading platform, and there, at times, he was able to read the stencilled addresses on the crates. Canada, India, New Zealand, Jamaica, and France, he read among foreign names. This, he knew, must be an export shipment being rushed off to various ships lying in different home ports, and, as he did not see a single address in England, he guessed that this particular day must be devoted entirely to foreign orders.

He already knew something about the Marsden bicycle. On the very day when Peter J. Mendley called on Sexton Blake, the detective had sent Tinker out to buy a Marsden and a Mendley.

"Get both machines," was his order, "and take them round to the garage. Then strip them to the frames. Get Jones or Farmer to help you. You are quite competent to make a comparison of the two, but get one of the others to check you up. It will be as well, too, for you to familiarise yourself with the Marsden before you go out of Slough."

Thus began Blake's campaign to try and discover what lay behind the price mystery of the Marsden. The business did not bear the earmarks of being a "long firm" fraud. A few inquiries were sufficient to show that the Marsden Cycle Co. stood very high financially.

They had a big credit balance in two banks, and their paper had a close discount value in the City. Moreover, Blake was able to ascertain that their purchases had been invariably met promptly, and that they had not in any single case asked for long terms, preferring to take all cash discounts that offered.

There was one possibility that Blake had in mind. This was a public issue of shares later on. He had known in the past of firms who had built up a big turnover through defensive advertising, and when their product had seemed well established had made a big public issue of shares, the promoters receiving large cash consideration for their interests in the parent company.

That was a step that only the future could show; at the present time there was no rumour of any such forthcoming issue by the Marsden people.

Once Tinker, disguised as a young workman, had left for Slough, Blake knew he could do nothing beyond his bank and City inquiries until he should hear from the lad. So he put the matter from his mind and gave his whole attention to Detective-inspector Thomas, of Scotland Yard, who, for some time past, had been coming to him to talk over a series of robberies in England and on the Continent that bore the earmarks of being the work of an international gang working along a special line.

The majority of these cases referred to banknote thefts and banknote swindles. At Brussels, in Belgium, for instance, the local branch of a big Paris bank had been swindled out of no less than two million francs by the presentation of a forged letter of credit. This was the first incident that set the Belgian and French police to work in real earnest, and it was not long before they began to see a definite connection between the Brussels affair and a dozen or so smaller frauds that had been occurring at different points on the Continent over a period of many months.

Until the unknown crooks had lifted this two millions from the bank in Brussels, the investigations had been merely routine. But now there was a definite clue. The letter of credit had been issued in Madrid, or rather, purported to have been issued there by a leading Spanish bank in favour of a Spanish merchant, whose name was beyond suspicion. This gentleman was travelling in France and Germany, and had with him a letter of credit, issued by the same bank.

It was a bold move to cash in on the forgery while he was actually travelling in the same countries where the crooks swung the swindle, for he was prominent enough to have his movements reported in the papers.

It was not, therefore, until some time elapsed that the first fraud was discovered. This quickly brought urgent inquiries from the Spanish bank, which produced such revelations that the police of Paris, Brussels and Berlin sat up with a shock. Scotland Yard was warned, and as further swindles were pulled off they were kept posted.

Then came the robberies. A famous jeweller in the Rue de la Paix was robbed of diamonds and pearls to the tune of nearly three million francs. Followed the robbing of a small but rich local bank at Dijon in France, where the thieves gained access by the simple expedient of stabbing the watchman in the back.

This occasion was a masterpiece of scientific safe-breaking. The most modern appliances were used to fuse away the armour-plate steel of the strong-room, and, disdaining the paper and silver, the thieves got away with the entire gold reserve of the bank. It was under the unofficial control of a big Paris bank that immediately came to the rescue, otherwise it must have closed its doors, with heavy losses to its depositors.

It would take a long catalogue to complete a list of the crimes which followed, and, so persistently consistent were the methods employed, that it became evident to the official police of the countries concerned, that the whole series could only be the work of a strong international organisation under one control.

Then came events which caused Scotland Yard to prick up its ears, for things were beginning to strike near home. Inspector Thomas had not sought Blake's aid. It was his custom to drop in at Baker Street and talk things over while he could improve the shining hour,' so to say, by absent-mindedly helping himself to a handful of Blake's choice partagas cigars. Thus, not long after Tinker's departure for Slough, his bulky figure and round, bluff countenance appeared in the consulting-room door.

"Come in—come in!" called Blake, continuing his work, but amusedly keeping an eye on the cigar cabinet. "What is it today?"

Thomas performed absolutely according to schedule. He laid aside his hat, sighed heavily, mumbled something about the day, sidled across to the table, and while gazing abstractedly out of the window transferred half a dozen partagas from the cabinet to his own pocket; then he sank into one of the deep saddle-back chairs, lit a cigar, and blew a ring ceilingwards.

Blake was smiling as he pushed the pad of paper from him and turned round.

"That lot is a little too green," he murmured.

Thomas blinked unintelligently.

"Huh?"

"I said that lot is a little green."

"Lot—what lot are you talking about? What is green?"

Blake helped himself to a cigar and gazed at it critically.

"Yes, a little green," he murmured once more. "Still not so bad at that."

Thomas refrained from comment. He was either strangely dense this morning or his mind was fixed on the matter that had brought him to Baker Street.

He put a hand in his pocket and took out a thick, red leather wallet. From this he extracted a folded banknote, which he handed to Blake.

"Just give that the once-over, will you, Blake?"

The detective took the note which, when he had unfolded it, he saw was an issue of the Bank of France for one thousand francs—or so it seemed. He laid it on a clean piece of blotting paper and, picking up a powerful reading glass, began to scrutinise the engraving. Very carefully he went over first one side then the other, after which he took it to the window and held it up to the light.

"A remarkable forgery," he announced at length. "The paper is perfect—must have been stolen from actual stock; the engraving and printing are beyond reproach; it would pass all but the most experienced eyes and fingers."

"What's wrong with it, then?"

"There is just one fault that I can detect for certain, although I am inclined to think a comparison with a genuine note might show a very slight difference in the shade of the violet ink in the lower right-hand corner. The fault of which I am sure, however, is the tail of the 'g' in the word 'egalité.' It is infinitesimal, but I am willing to wager it is a shade too long."

Thomas did not conceal his admiration.

"How the dickens you carry that stuff in your mind I don't know, but you are dead right. The tail of the 'g' in that word is too long, and you are right in saying the purple ink in the lower right-hand corner is a shade different from that in a genuine note of the same denomination. Here you are—here is a genuine flimsy; compare them."

He took out another note, and handed it to Blake. The latter spread it out and made comparison. He was human enough to feel a little glow of satisfaction at finding himself proved correct. He had studied the subject of forged banknotes over many years, had soaked in the subject from the manufacture of paper and inks to a mastery of the different schools of engraving, and had finished off his work by writing a small monograph on the subject, with an appendix in the back giving a list of all the notorious forgers over a period of two centuries.

"Where did you pick up the dud?" he asked at last.

"It was handed to me by the manager of the Paris and Calais Bank in the Haymarket. Their receiving cashier parted with just one million two hundred thousand francs in genuine ten thousand flimsies for an equivalent sum in these dud thousand franc notes."

"Whew! A nice little haul. When did this take place?"

"Yesterday."

"Any clue?"

"Nothing much. Two men appeared at the grill and placed a handbag on the ledge. They piled out the notes and asked for them to be exchanged into ten thousand franc notes of the Bank of France, as they wished to send a large sum in French currency abroad. The cashier didn't have the full amount for which they had asked, but said if they would return he would secure them from another bank. He could scarcely refuse them, for one of the men presented a card bearing the name of a Paris gentleman who was a very valued customer of the bank. They agreed and asked the cashier to take charge of the bag for them until they returned. There's nerve for you, Blake. They duly showed up again soon after two in the afternoon, and the exchange was concluded. This morning some of the notes they handed in were sent in exchange to an English bank, when it was discovered they were forgeries. The whole caboodle was then checked up, and every rag-tag bit of paper was a dud. It's the biggest trick of its kind that has been pulled off in this country for a long time past, and is only beaten by the stunt worked on the forged Letter of Credit in Brussels a few months ago."

"Do you suspect it to be the work of the same gang?"

"Well, if it isn't it was carried out by pupils of that crowd."

"Most interesting; but I take it you have not come to see me to get my opinion."

"I came because I know the manager of the Paris and Calais Bank is going to bring you into it."

17

"Ah! I had no idea—"

"Well, I know, because he told me. That's why I thought I would come along and have a palaver before you got to work. I—"

Thomas broke off as the telephone rang. "That may be the manager now," he added.

Blake nodded and, swinging round in his chair, reached for the instrument. The next moment he was listening to a voice at the other end of the wire, but it wasn't that of the bank manager.

CHAPTER 3.   The Mystery Gang.

IT was Tinker getting through from Slough.

He reported, as is already known, how he had secured work at the Marsden works without any difficulty, and that he was to begin on the job at the afternoon shift. He gave Blake the address of his lodgings and then, as Blake had no fresh instructions for him, he rang off.

Blake mentioned to Thomas that it was the lad, but he did not explain what he was doing nor where he had 'phoned from. Then he reverted to the subject they had been discussing.

"Has anything developed about that Sheffield business?" he asked as he lit a fresh cigar.

Thomas shook his head and frowned. Blake had touched a sore spot, for a serious crime had been committed in the great manufacturing city of the north some two weeks previously and, after struggling futilely with the problem for the better part of a week the local police had appealed to Scotland Yard.

This appeal should have been made the day of the crime, but a large proportion of the provincial police are jealous of their position, and not too eager to seek the aid of the superior knowledge and equipment of the Yard.

The case had been handed over to Inspector Thomas, and Blake knew that he had been in Sheffield almost constantly for the past ten days, and that he could not have been back in London more than twenty-four hours or so.

The crime itself was one of cold-blooded murder and robbery. The cashier of a big steel rolling firm had been shot dead in his office less than half an hour after his return from the bank with the week's payroll for more than two thousand hands. The raid was carefully planned and boldly carried out, for the office was full of clerks and typists when it took place.

The direct evidence was brief enough. Two masked and armed men entered the place, and while one of them held up the clerks with his automatic, the other pushed through to the cashier's office, where the latter was checking over the payroll with a junior clerk. He did not have a chance.

The robber shot him down without a word, and, threatening the young clerk with his gun, coolly swept all the money into the bag. Then the pair rushed out, and all that was known of their movements after that was that a powerful touring-car was seen dashing away from the gates of the mill. The haul was just over nine thousand pounds. It was this crime to which Blake was referring.

Thomas shook his head gloomily.

"I haven't struck a single thing," he confessed. "If those fellows in Sheffield had called us in sooner there might have been a chance, but you know what they are as soon as the Yard is mentioned."

"Has it occurred to you that it might be the work of the international gang we have been discussing—of them or some of their 'pupils' as you describe them?"

"I thought of that, but this haul was only nine thousand—only chicken-feed to that mob."

"I am not so sure of that, take that string of jewel robberies in France and Germany, yes, and in Belgium, too. Some of them totalled a large amount, but others were comparatively small; yet the Paris Surete is convinced that they are all linked together. Look here, Thomas, if this international gang does exist as is suspected—if it is a widespread organisation with its ramifications throughout Europe— then it is being conducted on strictly business lines.

"Take any big wholesale firm doing a legitimate form of trade. Name me any one you wish, and I'll show you what I mean."

Thomas looked at him in a puzzled way.

"I don't know what you're driving at, Blake, but if you want a name I'll give you one—Venters, the big shipbuilding people."

"Right. They manufacture all forms of steel castings, tubes, guns, armourplate, and, in fact every conceivable form of finished steel. They can turn you out a battleship complete, a cruiser or a submarine; they can build you a harbour fully equipped, or throw a gigantic bridge across the widest river; they can quote you within twenty-four hours for a finished railway system in any country; or they would not disdain to give you a price for a small dinghy if it came within the scope of their business. They would sell you a full cargo of nails or a single keg. Now don't you see what I am driving at?"

"You mean this international gang of thieves are ready to take anything that offers?"

"Exactly that. If they are organised on a strictly business basis, then the members must work on a drawing account and expenses. A general fund would have to be put in reserve for the protection of any members who might be caught—for legal expenses, and so on. And then dividends would have to be paid. In order to operate successfully they would have to be prepared to tackle small jobs as well as big; they would have to operate in the most catholic way, take a hand in every form of crime, and have on the staff experts in each class. I have been giving a lot of thought privately to this subject since I received a letter about a month ago from M. Dupuis, the Prefect of Paris, and the more I study the series of crimes in different countries the more I believe there to be a cold, business direction behind them. But there is something else, and, to my mind, it is the most important phase of the whole problem."

"What is that, Blake?" asked Thomas, looking up quickly.

Sexton Blake opened a drawer in his desk, and took out a sheet of foolscap paper on which Tinker had typed a long list of what Thomas found, on scrutinising them, made up a partial catalogue of the various crimes in France, Belgium, and Germany, which had been attributed by the Continental police to the same gang. Beside or beneath the brief details of each coup with its date were particulars of the nature of the swindle. Thomas read it, and handed it back.

"Well?"

Blake replaced the sheet in the drawer.

"You have just seen a partial list of the crimes which it is believed this gang has carried out. You have seen a catalogue which included the negotiation of forged banknotes, large and small swindles worked through the medium of forged cheques, bills of exchange and letters of credit; you have seen items representing jewellery stolen from a score of dealers in various countries, some amounting to enormous sums and others of much lesser value. Scotland Yard has been in close touch with the police of Paris, Brussels, and Berlin. I dare say you have even had communications from Vienna."

"Yes, we have."

"Very well. You have received all these particulars of swindles and robberies, but have you, in any one instance, been able to trace any of the stolen property to any of the known fences either on the Continent or in this country?"

Inspector Thomas cast a startled look at Sexton Blake.

"Er, why, now that you mention it, Blake. I don't believe we have. Of course," he added apologetically, "Scotland Yard hasn't a real chance yet. It is only recently that we suspected that gang of coming to England; but I don't recall that the Continental police have traced any of the stolen property."

"We will leave the notes out of it for the moment. I know that a large amount of the actual paper obtained by swindling and plain robbery has drifted back into circulation, but the path it has travelled has been so well covered that it has been impossible to trace back to the point where it was first released. But get to the other stuff—the stolen diamonds, pearls, emeralds, objets d'art, and so on—has any of that been traced? Not yet. But every known fence on the Continent has been given the third degree, as it were. Not one has spilled the beans because I don't believe they knew anything to spill."

"What the deuce are you driving at?"

"I am getting round to the point I made before—that this gang is as efficiently organised for its business as, say, the highly respectable firm of Venters whom you mentioned. And I have a hunch that they have a means of passing the loot along hidden channels into a central depot; where it will be melted down in the case of metal or re-cut in the case of precious stones or sold secretly in the case of objets d'art to some unscrupulous collector. If I am right, then you have an explanation why the other robberies are interlarded, so to say, by these swindles and frauds which bring in actual bank notes. Have you any record yet of Bank of England notes being part of these hauls?"

"Not yet; but there were a lot of forged Bank of England notes negotiated in Paris and Vienna."

"That is different, though it may have been the work of the same gang. I'll take a chance, and say that every really clever forger in Europe is on the staff of this organisation. Bank of England notes can be traced by their numbers; most of the Continental notes are like the American notes—they are more easily passed than ours, and the numbers form no check. But this criminal firm, if I may use the phrase, must have the sinews of war; hence the Pyramids, as Tinker would say. Now do you get my point?"

"I follow your meaning, but I don't see—"

Blake held up his hand.

"Paris, Brussels, Berlin, Vienna, and now Scotland Yard are all looking for the crooks. They have smoked out the best-known fences, it is true, but I'll wager you what you will that the most direct answer to the riddle lies along the other line I have mentioned. Find the means by which the gang is getting rid of the other stuff, and the central storage depot where the hauls are being collected and altered for disposal, find the channel by which they are being sent to that central receiving depot, and you will have the answer to what I am beginning to think is going to prove the biggest criminal turnover of modern times."

"Then why haven't you taken a hand? You say M. Dupuis has been in correspondence with you on the subject."

"When I am invited officially to do so I may consent. In the meantime, I pursue my own affairs, and watch."

"Well, the manager of the Paris and Calais Bank said he was going to get in touch with you."

Once more the telephone rang. Blake lifted the receiver and spoke. His words conveyed little meaning to Thomas, for they were, mostly monosyllabic; but when he hung up and turned back to his visitor there was a gleam in his grey eyes that had not been there before.

"You are right, Thomas; the manager of the Paris and Calais Bank has asked me if I can make it convenient to call on him at half-past two this afternoon,"

Out at Slough, Tinker would have thought the investigating of a mystery connected with the selling of bicycles a very tame business compared with what Blake and Thomas had been discussing. He never would have believed that the two could be in any way connected, nor that in that stupid difference in prices lay the key to a riddle that was to give Sexton Blake the hardest fight he had had for many a long day.

Monsieur Ferrand, the London manager of the Paris and Calais Bank, was a middle-aged gentleman verging somewhat on the corpulent, which suited well his immaculate dress and polished manners. He had come to London as a young man, and spoke English perfectly. His father had been a big shareholder—as was he now—and director in the Paris and Calais Bank, and through this influence young Ferrand had had access to the most influential financial circles in London, which despite the ravages of the war, is to-day, as it was then, the centre of the financial world.

He received Sexton Blake in his sumptuously-furnished private room where he installed his visitor in a luxurious easy chair and provided him with a cigar that was the equal of Blake's own choice partagas. Then when he had given instructions that on no account was he to be disturbed, he also lit a weed, and pressing the tips of the fingers of the right hand on the polished mahogany, regarded the detective.

"I asked you to come and see me, Mr. Blake, not because I have not every confidence in Scotland Yard, but because I want a certain matter investigated by someone who will not be handicapped by even a suspicion of red tape. We, that is the bank, have suffered a very heavy loss through one of the most daring swindles that has ever been perpetrated."

The detective inclined his head, but did not say that he already knew the principal details of the affair. It was not for him to disclose that an inspector from the Yard had confided in him.

"The amount we have lost is one million two hundred thousand francs," went on Ferrand. "A tidy sum even for a bank as rich as this. Shall I give you the details?"

"Please."

Forthwith the manager began, and gave Blake a description of the affair, which was, more or less, what Thomas had already told him. There were one or two unimportant points which had come up since, but which did not change the material facts, viz: that two men had entered the bank the previous day about half-past eleven in the morning and had requested the receiving cashier to accept one million two hundred thousand francs in Bank of France notes of one thousand francs each in exchange for an equal sum —less the small fee which would be exacted in such cases—of Bank of France notes of ten thousand francs each. Normally, in the case of strangers, such a large sum would not be accepted haphazard, but one of the men had handed in the card of a gentleman who was one of the best customers of the bank in Paris. On the back of the card was pencilled a brief introduction of one "M. Jaspar Benoist," and the scribbled signature was sufficiently like the copy in the signature-book at the bank to pass muster.

The manager then went on to tell Blake how there was not a reserve of sufficient ten thousand franc notes to meet the demand, and how the two men were requested to return later in the day when the exchange would be made. They had duly come back at half-past two in the afternoon and the business was completed. He added that they had left their own bag of notes in the care of the bank while they were gone.

"That alone was enough to disarm any suspicion, even if the card of the Paris customer had not been presented," he said, by way of explanation. "Everything seemed perfectly regular, and, of course, it never occurred to us to tamper with the bag. It was sealed temporarily and put in the vault against their return. It was not until we paid certain of those one thousand franc notes to an English bank against some of our cheques that were presented that it was discovered they were forgeries. As soon as the English bank advised us of this I had the whole sum checked. You can imagine my consternation, Mr. Blake, when it was found that every note was a forgery; there was not a single genuine note among the lot to act as camouflage. I shall give you one of those notes and a genuine note presently for you to make a comparison."

Again Blake inclined his head, but the cloud of smoke he blew out just then hid the faint flash of amusement that showed in his eyes. He thought it just as well not to mention that he had already had an opportunity of making such a comparison.

"I at once notified Scotland Yard," proceeded Monsieur Ferrand, "and Detective inspector Thomas was sent round, he now has the matter in hand, and seemed quite satisfied when I informed him that I intended to seek your aid as well. You will find it possible, I hope, Mr. Blake, to take up the investigation. I need not assure you that my bank will be generous in the matter of fees and expenses."

Blake made a gesture with one hand. "You say two men turned the trick, Monsieur Ferrand; I should like a description of them."

"I have anticipated that question. The receiving cashier prepared a written description from what he could remember of them for the benefit of Inspector Thomas, and I have had a copy made for you."

As he finished speaking, he opened a drawer and took out a sheet of typed paper. Handing this to Blake, he sat back and waited while the detective read what was written. This is how it ran:

"First man, the one who carried the bag and presented the card bearing name of Monsieur Acier, of Paris, was about six feet tall and very thin; ago about forty, with deep-set eyes so dark as to appear almost black, prominent nose, with pronounced bridge and thin, spreading nostrils. Baggy under the eyes, and hollows in the cheeks as if side teeth had been removed; front teeth prominent when he spoke and smiled; mouth partially concealed by dark moustache that was long and untidy of points, neck thin, hair dark brown, ears rather prominent. Was well-dressed in a dark blue suit, but not of English cut; linen, white and clean; wore a solitaire diamond ring on the third finger of his left hand; his hat was a black bowler; could not see his shoes while at the counter, and did not notice them when he walked out. Manners polished, and spoke French with a Parisian accent. Would say he was Parisian born.

"Second man was about five foot nine or ten, of somewhat nondescript appearance, and seemed but to accompany the other, for he did no talking. Rather stout, and dressed in a brown suit, not of English cut, wore a brown trilby hat. Was clean-shaven, and I think had brown eyes, but they may have been hazel; his brows were very heavy."

Blake glanced up when he had finished reading.

"Am I to keep this?"

"Your question means you accept the retainer?" said the manager, with a smile.

Blake nodded as he folded the sheet and placed it in an inside pocket.

"I think you may take it that my answer is 'Yes,' Monsieur Ferrand. Have you anything else to tell me?"

"Firstly, I will answer one question which Inspector Thomas asked and which you may also put. That is, whether I have any reason to suspect collusion between the two men who brought the forged notes and the receiving cashier."

"Yes, I would have wanted to know that."

"I have implicit faith in the receiving cashier. He is quite incapable of any such breach of trust. I have known him since he was a child; his father is a heavy shareholder in our bank and a director as well. The young man has a large independent fortune of his own."

"That seems to let him out," agreed Blake. "Have you been in touch with the gentleman in Paris—Monsieur Acier, I believe you said his name was?"

"Yes. I got through to him on the long-distance telephone just before lunch. He absolutely repudiates any knowledge of two such persons as I described, and assures me he never gave any card to them or to anyone else."

"Yet even if they had stolen it they had sufficient acquaintance with his signature to forge it?"

"Quite true; but they may have secured one of his cheques at some time or other."

"What is his business?"

"He is a stockbroker—a member of the Paris Bourse."

"Then it would be easy enough to get hold of one of his cheques on a small sale of shares."

"Yes. Now what questions occur to you, Mr. Blake?"

"I take it there is no trace of these two men since they walked out of the bank?"

"None whatever."

"We can rest assured that Inspector Thomas has already put the Yard machinery into motion. He will have the different railway termini watched as well as all the cross-Channel ports. I can do nothing in that direction. Tell me, Monsieur Ferrand, do you recall a swindle that was worked in Brussels a few months ago? I refer to a matter of two million francs in connection with a forged Spanish Letter of Credit."

"Indeed I do. In common with all other banks we were warned to be on the lookout for those persons."

"It has not occurred to you that there may be a connection between this affair and that?"

The banker looked suddenly thoughtful.

"I never thought of that, Mr. Blake. Tiens! I wonder if you have touched on something?"

Only by that one word of his native tongue did he betray his excitement

"We shall take measures to find out. I want you, please, to telegraph a description of these two men to that bank in Brussels and to ask them if it answers at all to that of anyone who presented the forged Spanish Letter of Credit. Request them to telegraph an answer as soon as possible."

The banker did not hesitate. Reaching over, he pressed a button in the desk, and, when a clerk entered, said curtly:

"Bring me the code-book and send my confidential secretary to me."

The clerk retired, but was back in a few moments with a green Bentley's code, and, on his heels, came a young woman with notebook and pencil. At a sign from the banker she seated herself at one end of his desk, and, with an efficiency and speed which showed that he had not forgotten his early training, Monsieur Ferrand dictated code message the translation of which he gave to Blake as he went along.

"You think that will answer, Mr. Blake?"

"Perfectly."

"Then get it away at once, Miss Greener. Instruct the cable clerk that all cables and telegrams are to be brought to me during the rest of the day without being opened."

"Very well, sir."

When she was gone Ferrand turned back to Blake.

"Just why did you think of that, Mr. Blake?"

Blake decided to take him into his confidence. Briefly he told him of the extraordinary series and variety of crimes that had been bothering the police of several countries for some months past. He explained his theory much as he had given it to Thomas, and, like the inspector, the banker wanted to know why he had not taken an active part in the investigation. Blake gave the same reason.

"Because I was not commissioned by any of the victims to do so, and, of course, the police would not call me in. But you have retained my services, Monsieur Ferrand, and if I can prove a connection between this swindle and that in Brussels, I shall strengthen my suspicions that they are but two incidents among many. I don't mind confessing it is because I hope to uncover some such connection that I am influenced to take a hand."

"Not forgetting our million odd francs," added the banker, with a smile.

"Not forgetting your million odd francs," echoed Blake as he rose. "You will let me know the moment you hear from Brussels?" he went on as he picked up his hat.

"Certainly. I shall take good care there is no leakage. I shall telephone you as soon as I decode the message."

"Thank you. I expect I shall be at Baker Street for the rest of the day."

With that Blake shook hands and was shown out by the banker in person. As he passed through the bank, Blake glanced at the young man who stood behind the window that was marked "Receiving Cashier." The young fellow wore a harassed look, but one look was sufficient for Blake to satisfy himself that it was very unlikely he had had any part in the swindle.

Back in the consulting-room he sat down and jotted down all the facts that he had gathered from Inspector Thomas and the banker. To these he attached the description of the two men who had worked the swindle, and thus was begun the dossier which was to grow dramatically as the days passed.

At half-past five that afternoon Blake drew in the first fish that entered the net he had cast. It was a telephone message from Monsieur Ferrand who read to him the telegram which had come from the bank in Brussels. It stated that the description of the taller of the two would fit, as far as could be remembered, one of the men who presented the forged Spanish Letter of Credit at that bank; but they were uncertain of the second man.

"What do you think of it, Mr. Blake?" asked the banker when he had finished reading.

"I think it quite sufficient to strengthen my theory," was Blake's answer. "At any rate, I am going ahead on those lines."

"And I am sure you have struck the right clue," agreed the banker. "Good luck to you, and let me know results."

"I'll keep in touch," promised Blake.

At half-past six the telephone rang again. This time it was Tinker sending through his first report from Slough. After stating that he had got through his first afternoon's work without incident, he spoke in a way that told Blake he was holding his lips close to the mouthpiece.

"I've seen the head of the Marsden Cycle Co., guv'nor," he murmured. "You'll get a shock when I tell you it is someone we know."

"Who is it, young 'un?" asked Blake sharply.

There was a slight pause; then in even lower tones:

"Listen carefully, guv'nor—it's George Marsden Plummer."

OUT of the gloom of the room came a whisper.

"Close the door!"

Into the dingy garret a figure had crept, and now, at the command, a hand moved backwards to push the rickety door that hung on one ancient hinge. Followed a scraping sound as the newcomer scuffed his way across the floor. He almost stumbled over a table, and again that whisper cut through the darkness.

"Have a care, you fool. Were you followed?"

"No; I waited at three points and watched. No one followed."

"Where is Pierre?"

"He is keeping watch."

"Have you locked the lower door?"

"Yes, and placed the bar as well."

"How will Pierre get in?"

"He will make the squeal of a rat in the alley; I will go down and admit him."

"Then if you are sure you were not followed light the lamp. But if anything happens you know what to expect."

The conversation had been carried on in French, but it was not until a match had been struck and the dirty oil-lamp lighted, one might have seen that, of the two persons now in the garret, one was a woman. It was she who had been waiting— she who had sent that first whisper cutting through the gloom; but one can't distinguish between the whisper of a man and a woman. The other was a man.

Not among all the sweepings of Paris would it have been possible to pick out two more disreputable-looking figures than this pair. Not even in the café of the "clochards" would one have seen worse rags. The woman's face was half-concealed by matted grey hair that fell down on either side, tangled and frowsy as if it had not known a comb or brush for many years.

Her bodice was but a makeshift garment of patched rags in a dozen different colours; her skirt was a filthy stained petticoat. Her eyes were black and intense as two live coals; they peered out at the man with a menacing threat that made him shiver as his own vapid gaze met hers. She might have been forty gone to seed through drug; she might have been seventy through the same reason.

The man was typical of the clochards, dirty, unkempt and with an evil sneer stamped on his filthy countenance. He was stooped and coughed harshly after one breath of the smoke from the match. In age he might have been put down as thirty or forty—either would have seemed fitting.

From a capacious pocket inside his rags he took out a loaf of bread and a bottle of red wine. He cut chunks off the loaf with a clasp-knife that lay on the table, and which, in contrast to almost everything else in the garret, was polished clean. Then he drew the cork of the wine with a corkscrew that opened from the back of the knife, and, setting that before the woman, went to a cupboard, from which he took two tumblers, also remarkable for their cleanliness.

At a gesture from the woman, he seated himself. She pushed a share of the bread towards him while he poured the wine; then the two began to eat, making no attempt at conversation while they did so.

At last, however, the simple repast was finished. The man took away the empty glasses, and, with the remains of the bread, placed them in the cupboard. The woman lit a cigarette from a yellow packet, while her companion selected a "Caporal" from a blue packet. Each tube was lit over the top of the lamp chimney.

Thus they sat smoking in silence for the better part of twenty minutes, the eyes of the man fixed on the smoky flame of the lamp, those of the woman dividing their attention between the smoke that curled from her cigarette and the man. At last she ground the glowing ash into the top of the deal table.

"What time is it?"

Before he could reply there came through the dirty but complete curtain that covered the sloping window a faint squealing sound. At once the man was on his feet, his cigarette ground into the wood beside the other. In another swift movement he had blown out the lamp, and then a faint scraping sound followed as he made his way to the door.

The woman did not move until she heard the faint squeak of the door, and allowed an interval of about two minutes for him to descend the three flights of rickety stairs that she knew lay between the garret and the street. But at the end of that brief period of time she thrust a hand beneath the voluminous petticoat and drew out a small, fully-loaded automatic with a cutoff barrel which she held in the folds of the skirt. That was all—she just continued to sit and wait.

Presently there was a faint sound in the short hall outside, and once more her whisper cut through the darkness.

"Close the door."

The slight squeak sounded again, and there followed the scraping of feet as someone crossed the room. A match was struck and the lamp lighted. As the wick flamed up it revealed the countenance of the same man who had entered before. But the woman's eyes were not for him. She was peering through her matted grey hair at the figure that was standing just inside the door. Now he came forward, and, after a formal bow towards the woman, a bow that might have been sincerely respectful or merely ironical, he coolly drew out a chair and sat down.

Although his face was unquestionably of the Apache type, he was very differently dressed from his two companions. His clothes were new and of the exaggerated cut of the Bellevue district; his shoes had glistened like polished mirrors as he crossed the room; his linen was of a blatant pink, and in his hand was a typical Apache cap, which now he dropped on the floor. He shot a quick glance at the woman, and took out a packet of cigarettes.

"Well, what is your report?" And now her voice was strangely in contrast to that she had used before; it was the voice of a young woman, vibrant, decisive.

And at the sound both her companions moved nervously.

"It is done, madame," replied the Apache. "I obeyed orders. I waited outside the bank until my friend appeared. He was able to give me the information at last; for have I not waited each day for a full week?"

"Never mind that. You have been well paid. Get on with your report."

He shot a furtive look at her, but it was plain that she held those two on a leash which they feared to break.

"The time is ripe, madame. He left the bank at a quarter to six, carrying a black leather bag. A quick hand might have snatched it then, but the streets were crowded. I was ready to follow. He entered his own limousine. I have written down the number. He stopped at the Cercle Royal, his club, for about half an hour. He carried the bag into the club and brought it out with him. Then he continued to a building of flats in the Champs Elysees—the number is 87bis. He paid a visit to a flat on the second floor, he carried the bag in with him and brought it out again when he left at the end of an hour; but I am thinking, madame, that he may have left the contents there."

"You are not paid to think. Go on."

The Apache risked a shrug, but a second later his eyes widened and his jaw dropped open as he found the snubbed barrel of a blue automatic jammed under his nose.

"Just once more, Pierre, and you won't be interested in anyone's movements—ever again. Go on!"

"He drove up the Champs Elysees and across the Place de l'Etoile to the Avenue Marceau. Alors! He entered the mansion where he lives. I waited until nine, but he did not come out again. Then I went round to the back, where I managed a word with Cravette. He informed me that monsieur had dined at home, and had announced that he would be busy in his library all the evening; he was not to be disturbed. Then, madame, I came here and gave the signal."

"Cravette understands what he has to do?"

"Yes, madame."

"Will the door be locked?"

"He assures me it will be opened when he takes monsieur's tray at eleven o'clock. Monsieur has the habits of the English— he takes the vin d'écosse (whisky) before retiring."

"At eleven—that is well. It is now ten. There is no time to be lost. Go you, Armand, and tell Jean to drive the car to the head of the alley. We will get out at the street beyond the mansion in the Avenue Marceau. I know that street by night; it is dark. You, Pierre, will remain on guard at the back; Armand will come inside with me and do what is necessary. Swift work, Armand, and no clumsiness. You understand?"

"Yes, madame."

"Then go."

The two men rose at her bidding, and again Pierre bowed; but this time there was not the faintest chance for one to stamp the effort with irony. It was wholly respectful. As for Armand, he simply nodded his head and slouched across the room. He was of his class and a killer; he made no effort at being anything else.

This time the woman did not put out the lamp, but sat smoking a fresh cigarette until a sound came from below that might have been the frighteued squeal of a rat. Then, however, she rose swiftly, and, still clutching the automatic, walked quickly to the door. Closing it, she set a chair against it, and turned to a heavy wooden chest that stood against one wall. What followed was as extraordinary a metamorphosis as one could imagine; it was far more than the emergence of a brilliant insect from the chrysalis of a grub. At one moment there was in that attic a hag of repulsive appearance; when the change was complete there stood forth a glowing figure of youthful beauty clad in a dark blue tailored suit that could only have come from one of London's smartest ladies' tailors, with small dark blue cloche hat to match and black, well-made shoes on dainty feet. On the chest lay a rich mink coat, and against the fur was a black silk mask.

For a few moments the girl, for she was no more, stood in the centre of the garret gazing about her, dainty nostrils quivering in distaste at the squalor. Now, as she moved towards the light, her face was fully revealed, a face of wondrous beauty with black eyes burning with extraordinary vitality. Suddenly she caught up the mink cloak and wriggled her shoulders into it; the black silk mask she slipped into an inner pocket; the blunt-nosed automatic she thrust into the side-pocket of the blue serge coat. Then she leaned over and blew out the lamp.

Out of that dingy lair she moved, a thing of lightness and grace that defied description—a creature of the world of softness and luxurious sensuousness. This it was that floated rather than walked along the dark, cobbled alley—a bird of paradise emerging from the depths of a foetid jungle.

And it was the bird of paradise! It was Vali Mata-Vali, the adventuress and partner in crime of the notorious criminal, George Marsden Plummer.

At the top of the alley a closed limousine was waiting. It would, indeed, have been a strange vehicle for the hag of the attic to enter; but its sumptuous appointments were eminently in accord with the fashionably-dressed girl who slipped into its dim interior.

She had the wide, deep back seat all to herself. In the garret Pierre and Armand might be seated at the same table with the creature of the matted hair and rags; but here they were reduced to their correct level, and, under these conditions, one look of Vali Mata-Vali's eyes was more potent than any loaded automatic. She was dealing with the scum of the sewers, and knew it; but she hadn't a qualm about her capacity to handle them.

Nor did she give them even a thought as the car drew away from the top of the alley and took its way by devious narrow streets into the

Rue Delambro which would bring them into the Boul' Mich. She was not even thinking just then of the dangerous game she was playing that night —as dangerous a trick as she had ever attempted to turn without the moral and physical support of Plummer.

Her mind was dwelling, rather, on Plummer, for the master criminal was the one who held her heart and soul and body in the hollow of his big, capable hands— had held her thus ever since that purple night in Morocco when he had climbed to her in the harem by means of a silken ladder which she had lowered to him.

Sakr-el-Droog he had been then—Sakr-el-Droog, the Hawk of the Peak, but no longer captain of the front line troops of Abdel-Krim, the Lion of the Rif. Abdel-Krim had fallen and surrendered to the French. Only too well did George Marsdon Plummer know what would be his fate did he follow his leader. Abdel-Krim would be spared and placed in captivity, as, indeed, he was sent a little later to Madascar; but Sakr-el-Droog would be stuck up against a mud wall and shot.

So he had vanished in the wide desert, and then on that wonderful night when the moon washed the sands to silver he had climbed to that scented harem where he found the most wonderful vision in green silk that he had ever dreamed existed.

It was Plummer's Waterloo; never before, had he worked with a partner of either sex. Always he had played a lone hand, and therein had lain safety. But not for a single moment did he regret his yielding that night. Vali Mata-Vali, strange blend of East and West—sometime temple girl in the great temple that stands by the Gate of the Tiger in Canton and which takes its name from the hills of Eternal Purity which lie white-capped against the blue in the distance; later spy, actress, dancer and the idol of Paris, where she was christened the Bird of Paradise.

Then that journey into Morocco for the sole purpose of finding Sakr-el-Droog, of whom she had heard so much, and that night of moon and blossoms and heady scents.

Since then they had roamed the world, sometimes bringing off a daring coup that had kept them in luxury for many a long day; at other times fleeing from the wrath of their most persistent enemy, Sexton Blake. Yet never once had she regretted it; nor was there any other living man for whom she would have clothed herself in those filthy rags which were necessary an a disguise in this game which she and

Plummer had been playing for months past —the biggest, most widespread, most colossal scheme on which they had yet embarked.

Thus her thoughts as the limousine sped down the Boul' Mich and; crossing the Pont St. Michel, turned past the cathedral of Notre Dame. But as they swung into the Rue de Rivoli and approached the Place de la Concorde, she shook her thoughts from her with a little smile that none could see in the gloom that surrounded her.

Ahead lay the test, the prize for which she had been planning patiently ever since Plummer had put her in charge of the Paris end of the business. She must, at any cost, pull it off successfully. If she succeeded the result would stagger Europe when it was known— would set the police of five capitals by the ears. If she failed—at that thought she made a tiny clicking sound with her tongue and shook her head—she would not fail.

Monsieur Etienne Coppot had been for many years one of the best known figures in the banking world of Paris. Few persons knew that before the war, he had occupied no more responsible position than that of exchange clerk in one of the brokerage firms attached to the Bourse. His exact participation in the war is uncertain, but one could date his first appearance as a financier during that period when the French franc threatened to go the way of the German mark and the Russian rouble.

Coppot made money in exchange speculation—a lot of money— and then, as is so easy in France, he opened his own private bank. Where he had kept his knowledge of human nature until he was nearly forty years of age one can only guess; he certainly had not shown any marked psychological insight as an exchange clerk, but when he launched forth on his own, as the saying goes, he rapidly built up an enormous business through the simple process of offering a much higher rate of interest than any of the old established and sound banks in Paris.

A financial snowball will add to its girth quicker than any other kind. Human greed, the inborn desire to get something for nothing, the lure of the prize for a comparatively small outlay—those were the ingredients with which Etienne Coppot compounded his financial cocktail, and it was not long before the Coppot banking firm had its branches in every provincial centre throughout France.

The knowledgeable ones in the money world looked askance at Coppot and his methods; but the great mass of people were blinded by the lure of high interest and the additional oportunity which the Coppot bank offered its patrons of gaining a fortune by conducting a free drawing in prize bonds once every month. It was a grand and simple scheme which was quickly followed by others of Coppot's kidney, but their competition was more of an advertisement for Coppot than a hindrance, for his organisation was widespread, and it was he who had initiated the scheme. He was shrewd enough to see that substantial prizes and premiums were paid judiciously in different parts of the country. What did it matter if a few hundred thousand francs were given away? Didn't it bring in millions in return?

Yet no management of money can go on for ever under such artificial conditions. The law of supply and demand the money rates of the ruling banks such as the Bank of England, the Bank of France, the Federal Reserve Bank of America, and so on hold the scales finely balanced and thus when the inward flow began to lessen to a mere dribble, when the prizes and bonuses had to be cut down, and when a few disgruntled depositors withdrew their money, Etienne Coppot read the signs aright. The arrow was falling back to the earth.

Therefore, he got ready to stand from under. The remoter parts of South America began to exercise a strange fascination upon him, and more particularly a certain republic which, at that time, had no extradition treaty with France. But he moved cautiously. Slowly, but surely, he gathered in a bit here and a bit there—eased payments in one direction and another until the bearer securities and cash in his secret safety deposit box grew to a very large sum.

Yet he was shrewd enough to realise that he must continue that part of his business which was legitimate banking until he was ready to make his dash. At Bordeaux, a private yacht was waiting to put to sea at a moment's notice. His papers were made out to the name he intended adopting in place of Etienne Coppot. When he had raked in another million francs he would be ready, for he was determined to arrive in the land he would adopt with a cash capital of ten million francs in funds that would present no difficulties of negotiation.

It is odd what tiny straws will sometimes set into motion vast forces which not the most far-seeing can anticipate. Etienne Coppot may or may not have heard of the notorious criminal, George Marsden Plummer; he had certainly heard of and seen Vali Mata-Vali when, as an actress and dancer, the rage of Paris, she was known as the Bird of Paradise. But even if he had given any thought to either of the two at that time he would hardly have connected Plummer with an occasional Bill of Exchange on the Marsden Cycle Co., of Slough, Bucks, England, which passed through his bank for collection against shipments made to that firm by a French manufacturer of bicycle frames. It was unlikely that these bills ever came under the personal notice of Etienne Coppot.

It was Vali Mata-Vali who tipped Plummer off that the Coppot bank was rotten beneath its skin of prosperity. Acting in Paris as Plummer's agent for his French activities, she had built up an extraordinarily efficient espionage organisation. Occasionally she would slip into England quietly and confer with Plummer, but more often the master criminal would steal across to Paris, and there the two would plan the next coup.

It was thus that the Spanish Letter of Credit fraud in Brussels had been engineered; it was on one of these visits that Plummer had suggested, and Vali carried out, the big robbery of jewels in the Rue de la Paix.

For it was George Marsden Plummer who was behind the whole series of crimes which was exercising the keenest police minds of Europe—had built up an organisation that was more ambitious than any he had ever attempted before, and was of so subtle a nature that it was to be a long time before the whole secret should be revealed. But learning the secret was one thing; laying Plummer by the heels was another.

It didn't matter two straws to Plummer whether Coppot was a crook or not. Plummer had never been worried by any fine ethics on such points. It was a case with him of "dog eat dog" and the police grab the other man. And so when Vali Mata-Vali began to send along bits of information that showed how the wind was blowing, he didn't ask her how she got it; he only filed it away in a secret place and told her to keep her finger on the pulse of the Coppot banking activities.

And on this night, when the old hag of Montparnasse sat in her garret waiting for Armand, the apache, to come and make his report, she was ready for quick action. One spy inside the bank and Cravette, the butler, as accomplice inside the mansion in the Avenue Marceau, was how she followed Coppot's movements.

If her information was correct, then this night would be Etienne Coppot's last in Paris. The one weak link in the whole fabric she had built up was Coppot's friend, on whom he had called on his way home. For Vali Mata-Vali knew that it was big intention to clear out that very night. She knew all about the secret safety deposit box—she knew that he had already emptied it that day and that he had taken every sou from the bank after closing time that afternoon. Would he have all this loot at the mansion? He had carried the bag into the flat in the Champs Elysees. Had he left any or all of the money at the flat he had visited? That was one thing Vali had been unable to learn. But she had to take that chance, and when the big limousine drew up in the dimly-lit side street just beyond Coppot's mansion she was ready to stake her hazard.

It was Armand who guided her and Pierre down the narrow tradesmen's alley than ran at the back of the big houses. But when he had given the signal and Cravette, the swarthy Provencal butler, had opened a cellar door, it was the apache whom she left outside on watch. She could trust him only so long as she held him at the end of a gun; but Pierre, the clochard, would do her bidding to the letter. One never knew what fool break Armand might make if he guessed that ten million francs was at the end of the visit; Pierre would ask for only enough to indulge in an absinthe bout. As for Cravette, he had worked for Plummer before, and knew what price he would pay if he tried to double-cross him.

Vali Mata-Vali stepped into the gloom of the cellar and then moved quickly to the right, where she stood against the wall, her slim fingers gripped about the butt of her automatic. In his hand Cravette was carrying a small flashlight that had been shaded, and against this masked glare she could see Pierre's hunched shoulders as he lurched in through the door. Then Cravette whispered something to Armand and closed the door.

Without a word to Vali he turned, and as he moved forward she laid fingers on Pierre's arm.

"You next," she whispered.

The clochard moved ahead obediently, with Vali bringing up the rear. They kept on along a passage until Cravette came into another cellar, a clean, bare apartment with a single rough bench against the stone wall.

"It will be necessary to wait here, mam'selle," he whispered to Vali. "It is when monsieur rings for his whisky."

She nodded.

"How long now?"

"At any moment, or perhaps later. It is impossible to tell. He has been locked in the library ever since dinner."

"He has not summoned you?"

"Not once."

"Has anybody called?"

"None, mam'selle."

"What about the other servants?"

"Monsieur himself sent them to bed."

"That is excellent. You did not have to make the suggestion?"

"Only to monsieur. I told him if he was to be engaged all the evening I should be on duty, so he instructed me to send the others to their rooms."

"Has he done any packing?"

"He has two bags in the room off the library, where he sleeps when engaged late. It seems, as mam'selle says, that he is planning to go away. But he has said nothing, and he can't take much in those two bags."

"That indicates nothing. He has sent what he needs ahead to wait for him. Has the telephone rung this evening?"

"Not once. The house exchange is in the hall. I must have heard it, for monsieur has not asked me to change the switch to the library."

"All right. Now get this straight, Cravette. When he rings, you will take the tray. You will leave the door a little ajar so that Pierre can get in. You will stand between monsieur and the door so that Pierre can draw close. Then you will stand aside. Is that clear?"

"Entendu, mam'selle."

"Come closer, Pierre."

The clochard bent his head so Vali Mata-Vali could whisper in his ear.

"You have heard Cravette's instructions?"

"Oui."

"You know your part?"

"To a degree, mam'selle."

She handed him the automatic. Then she touched his right temple with the tip of a finger.

"Just here Pierre.

"Just there," he whispered.

"Once only, Pierre."

"Once only, mam'selle."

"And not too far away, Pierre. There must be marks of the powder, if possible."

"Entendu, mam'selle."

She drew back and sank down on the bench. But scarcely had she done so when, upstairs somewhere, there sounded the trilling of a bell, Cravette turned expectantly.

"It is he," came his whisper.

Vali rose at once and pushed Pierre's shoulder.

"Go."

Cravette led the way through a door to a flight of stairs. Up these they went in single file until they came into a kitchen. From here the butler led them to a small pantry where, on a tray, stood a bottle of whisky of a well-known Scots brand, a tall cut-glass tumbler and a siphon of soda. A small silver salver had a few biscuits laid on it.

Picking this up, Cravette assumed the manner of his position and, pushing open a green baize-covered door, stepped into a softly-carpeted hall. He passed the door of a dining-room and then entered a large, beautifully-furnished square hall in which mellow light was diffused through an amber silk Chinese shade. At the far end Vali could see the heavy plate glass of the inner vestibule door, and, through these panels, the wrought-iron grill of the main portals beyond. Three closed doors along the long side showed the position of the main salons and on the right another closed door communicated with the library where their intended victim sat waiting for his night-cap.

Coppot had evidently unlocked the door before ringing, for when the butler knocked and heard his master's "Entrez!" the door yielded readily enough. He did not open it wide, just enough to permit him to enter, and when he had taken one look through at the man who sat at a desk, his back to the door, Pierre, the clochard, slid in as well. From the hall outside came forth a slim hand which gripped the knob and drew the door almost closed.

But Vali Mata-Vali did not need actually to witness what took place in that room during the next few moments. She could picture Cravette moving towards his master, the tray held ready to set on the desk. She could imagine Coppot turning his head briefly to nod to Cravette; and she could visualise Pierre stealing closer and closer, taking advantage of the angle of Coppot's position and Cravette's bulk to reach his objective without being seen.

She could see Cravette bend over so that the upper part of his body would cut off the rest of the angle of Coppot's view, then she could picture the hand of the killer come up and slide in under Cravette's elbow until—

Crack!

Just one sound put a period to her visions. Even with the door not quite closed she had scarcely heard it in the hall, for she had taken pains to have the weapon fitted with a silencer. Followed a soft thud, then she pushed the door open and gazed at the scene that confronted her, Pierre had not bungled the job!

CHAPTER 5. Meet M. Thibaud.

TWO evenings after securing his job at the Marsden works, in Slough, Tinker would have come up to London to make a personal report to Blake, but when he telephoned and got Mrs. Bardell on the wire, he learned, somewhat to his surprise, that Blake had left that afternoon for Paris.

"The master said as 'ow you was to stay there," she informed him.

"Did he say how long he would be gone?" he asked impatiently.

" 'E didn't know—'e says 'e'll be back when I sees 'im, but you 'as to ring up heach day to find out."

"All right," grumbled the lad. "You tell him as soon as he gets back that I'll ring up in the evenings—can't manage it during the day; and tell him, too, that I have something to report."

With that he closed off and wandered down the street to a billiards saloon, wondering what had taken Blake abroad at such short notice, and peeved that he had been left kicking his heels at Slough, even if he was keeping an eye on George Marsden Plummer.

He did not see how Blake's journey could have anything to do with Plummer. Nor did he know yet that Plummer was no longer in Slough. He had not seen the master criminal all that day, but thought little of it; he figured he would see him about the factory the following morning, and thus keep a check on his movements.

What he had to report to Blake was not looming as very important in his mind. Blake had instructed him to keep a close tally on all goods coming into and going out of the factory. During those two days Tinker had seen enough to convince him that a perfectly legitimate business was being done, for a constant stream of crated machines was being shipped to every part of the British Isles, as well as to dozens of points abroad, and an equally large stream of frames and parts kept flowing into the receiving warehouses.

Not a single glance, not a whisper did he intercept that could have been interpreted in any way but on the level. The workmen were perfectly contented with their pay, and every man an expert at his particular job. They had been drawn from every part of the country and didn't bother their heads about the selling price of the Marsden bicycle. And the lad had to confess that an excellent machine was being turned out. There was no faking of parts; every item was just as represented.

Then where was the "nigger in the wood-pile" if, as Peter J. Mendley suspected, something of the sort existed. Or was it possible that Plummer had at last turned to honest ways? Tinker did little more than give this idea a fleeting thought. Could the leopard change his spots, he asked himself?

Through discreet inquiry he found out where Plummer was living. He had taken a large house about two miles out of Slough— which he called Marsden Manor— to which, as far as Tinker could discover, he went each evening when the factory was closed. The lad had not had an opportunity yet to investigate things in that direction, but he was determined to have a shot at it before long.

That, and details of the incoming frames and parts were the chief item of his report; so, since he couldn't reach Blake, he could only proceed along lines suggested by developments. He couldn't guess that Blake had gone to Paris owing to a financial crash there that had swept thousands of people to ruin, and the repercussions of which had reached even as far as London.

The Paris press, and, to a lesser extent, the London paper, had contained particulars of the suicide of Etienne Coppot of the Coppot Bank, and following that, the central house in Paris as well as the numerous branches throughout the country had been closed. The London agents, a reputable firm of private bankers, had been badly hit by the affair, and while meeting all the Coppot "paper" in London out of their private resources, had asked Blake to proceed at once to Paris in company with one of their partners in order to prepare an official report and to ascertain if anything could be saved out of the wreck.

By the time Blake reached Paris the press had secured further details, and after the fashion of some of the evening papers, had a lurid story to tell the home-going Parisian.

Someone in the know had talked. Coppot's position was laid bare. It was stated that for months past he had been quietly accumulating an enormous sum from the bank's resources in order to flee the country, but that he must have speculated heavily with this money, and when he realised that he was on the eve of a crash had committed suicide.

There were details of his mode of life, of his own huge mansion in the Avenue Marceau; of his young fiancée; of the fleet of motor cars in his garage; and of the yacht which waited at Bordeaux.

It was the captain of the yacht, with two months' wages due to him, who spilled the beans about that. As soon as he told his story there was a howl that sounded from one end of France to the other. There was an uproar in the Chamber of Deputies; there was a violent article in the "Matin" which demanded an immediate tightening up of the lax banking laws of the country. In the provinces crowds gathered before the Coppot banking premises, and when no money was forthcoming they smashed the windows, climbed through and demolished everything they could lay their hands on.

The same would have happened in Paris, but for a strong police cordon that was strung round the building. Another police cordon was necessary about the mansion in the Avenue Marceau. Thus the position when Sexton Blake left the Carlitz Hotel in the Rue de Rivoli and made his way to the Prefecture to call upon M. Dupuis, the Prefect of Paris.

This was about eleven in the morning. He had left the junior partner of the London banking firm, Mr. Bridges, to go on to the Coppot premises and try and discover how far the official investigators had got with their work.

After a discussion of casual things, it was only natural that Blake and M. Dupuis should settle down to a talk about the various matters which had been the subject of recent correspondence between them—that is, the strange series of crimes and frauds which had taken place during the preceding months. The Chief of the Surete had nothing new to report, and Blake's own investigations were still in too much a state of flux for him to commit himself to any definite theory.

"I have an idea on which I am working," he confessed however. "You have heard, of course, about the fraud practised on the London branch of the Paris and Calais Bank?"

"Yes; the head office here reported to us and we have interviewed Monsieur Acier, whose name, you will recall, was used by the swindlers,"

"Yes, I saw the card which they presented. I am assured by the manager of the branch in the Hay market that the pencilled signature was sufficiently like the copy they have of M. Acier's signature in their book, that it passed unquestioned."

"Acier has, at our request, been through all his recent transactions, but we have learned nothing. He is a broker in a large way, and hundreds of cheques pass through his offices every day. It was like looking for a needle in a haystack. It is this matter which has brought you to Paris?"

"No. I have come over with the partner of a London banking firm to see what we can discover about the Coppot disaster. They acted as Coppot's London agents, and were pretty badly hit, although they have plenty of resources with which to meet their liabilities. I should be grateful if you would grant an interview to Mr. Bridges before he returns to London."

"Of course; you know I will do anything to oblige. But I am afraid you will draw a blank in the Coppot business. It is about as rotten a banking scandal as we have had in France for a century, and that is saying something. Some of the less responsible papers are already referring to it as a second 'Mississippi Bubble'."

Blake's smile was a little grim.

"As bad as that, is it?"

"The total defalcations look like going as high as a hundred million francs. Coppot had his organisation spread from one end of France to the other. It is extraordinary how people continually get swindled by these fellows. He paid such high rates of interest that even the most ignorant should have smelled something wrong. But greed is blind. He worked it very cunningly, paying prizes and bonuses as well, and, of course, those who received the plums drew in hundreds of others.

"Will any dividend be paid?"

"They haven't found enough loose cash or securities yet even to pay the outstanding wages of the staff."

"So when he knew the crash must come he blew his brains out."

"That seems the way of it."

Blake looked up quickly.

"Is there any doubt?"

The prefect shrugged and spread out his hands.

"It looks simple enough, but Thibaud has asked specially to be allowed to handle the affair."

Blake's interest deepened at mention of Thibaud. Emile Thibaud was the crack man at the Surete despite a most simple, guileless exterior which had been the downfall of the cleverest crooks in France. He had a knowlcdge of the underworld that was unequaled, and apart from the unassuming life he led with his family at Becon les Bruyeres, a suburb of Paris, his hobby was reading and re-reading the dossiers in the library at the Surete.

Blake had worked with him on more than one occasion in the past, and was asking himself why, if Coppot had committed suicide, as the prefect said, Thibaud should want to be bothered with the case. It seemed more like a routine job to be passed on to a less responsible official.

M. Dupuis must have guessed something of what was in the English detective's mind, for he smiled.

"Perhaps I can give you a hint as to why Thibaud is keen," he said, his eyes still twinkling. "Like so many of us who chase the crooked stalks, Blake, he is a child when it comes to money. And I have reason to believe that he was stung in the Coppot crash."

Blake saw nothing remarkable in the slang expression used by his vis-à-vis, for M. Dupuis spoke English, classic and colloquial, as if he had been born and educated in England. He appreciated what was just said, for he knew that Thibaud was always grumbling about his bad luck in investments.

"Anyway, you can ask Thibaud," went on M. Dupuis. "He may be able to give you a tip as to what the investigators have found so far. I will see if he is in his room. You will lunch or dine with me before you return? I want to have another talk with you about those other matters. It is a mystery to me how they are getting rid of the loot. We have put the probe again and again into every likely 'fence,' but haven't found the slightest thing. I refer more particularly to the jewels stolen in the Rue de la Paix robbery."

"Have you traced any of the money yet?"

"Some of the notes secured in that Brussels swindle have come to light, but they must have passed through scores of different hands. We trace them first in one direction, then another and another until the whole web becomes so confused we can't disentangle it. I tell you, Blake, there is a master brain behind them—one brain if, as you suspect, they are all linked up together."

"I make that statement with every reservation," said Blake slowly. "I have collected a few items which, so far, only show a very disjointed and confused picture, but we may strike the key bit of the puzzle before long. Do you mind if I discuss it with Thibaud?"

"Not at all; he has the matter in hand here. I'll ring now."

When Thibaud carried Blake off to his own room, the latter lost no time in putting his question direct.

"What makes you suspect that Coppot's death was not suicide?"

"Aha! Who says that Thibaud suspects?"

"The prefect informs me that you asked for the case to be given to you. Emile Thibaud does not waste his time in simple suicides."

"Oho! Did the chief tell you as well that Emile Thibaud had lost good money in the Coppot smash?"

Blake smiled his agreement.

"Alors! Is that not enough, mon ami?"

"Not for Thibaud," returned Blake equably. "Confess, my friend—you have other reasons."

"Why are you interested?"

"I am interested in the financial smash. I will explain."

Blake told how he had come to Paris with Mr. Bridges, of the London banking firm, in order to try and discover what he could about Coppot's private movements and life for some time preceding his death while he—Bridges—followed the work of the financial investigators.

"You would care to visit the mansion in the Avenue Marceau?" asked Thibaud when he had finished.

"Most assuredly, if you will be so kind."

"I will take you. You have, of course, read what the papers had to say?"

"Yes—both the Paris and London Press."

"I, Thibaud, have discovered one or two things. You will learn the same particulars from the financial investigators, and then can draw your own conclusions. It is believed that Coppot had collected a large sum of money in readiness for his projected flight. It must have amounted to many millions of francs. And I have got hold of a young clerk who has told me —things. It is said that Coppot made heavy speculations before his death, but this I do not believe, for I have had many conversations with Monsieur Acier, whose name may have been mentioned to you by Monsieur Dupuis."

"Yes, he spoke of M. Acier in connection with another matter."

"Aha! The affair of the Paris and Calais Bank, hein? So you have an interest in that as well, mon ami?"

"I am investigating it," confessed Blake.

"Well, M. Acier has been making careful inquiries. He is one with wide connections on the Bourse. But, aside from a few trifling transactions, he can find nothing that can be traced to Coppot."

"Then you believe that Coppot had a good deal of embezzled

money and securities in his possession at the time of his death?"

"What did he do with them?"

"What about his friend in the Champs Elysees?"

"His fiancée? I am satisfied that he gave her no very large sum. I had a talk with her before she retired to Enghien. She said as little as possible, but she confessed that he had visited her early in the evening on which he had met his death and told her to be ready to leave Paris the following day. She understood that they were going abroad, where they were to be married, and from what he said she believed that he had plenty of money in hand. What do you think of that?"

"If that is so, then it is certainly odd that he should commit suicide a few hours after," remarked Blake thoughtfully, "I have read the evidence contained in the Press reports. Was it fairly accurate?"

"It was officially sanctioned. I will recapitulate, mon ami. Here is Etienne Coppot. He leaves his bank shortly after his usual time, and from the evidence which we have been able to collect we can prove that he carried with him a large bag. He drove to his club, the Cercle Royal, where he partook of his usual aperitif and conversed with his friends. He was in high spirits, so I am assured. He still had the bag with him when he left his club and proceeded to 87bis, Avenue des Champs Elysees, the residence of his fiancée. He remained with that lady for some time, and then drove straight to his own hotel in the Avenue Marceau."

"Yes, the papers said all that," murmured Blake.

"And I have proved it, every step. What happened after he reached home? He dined alone, and then entered his library after giving orders to his butler that he was on no account to be disturbed until he rang. With his own lips he ordered all the servants but the butler to retire, and then, closing the door of his library, he locked the door on the inside. The butler retired to the pantry, where he sat reading, smoking and sometimes dozing until a few minutes after eleven o'clock, when his master rang."

"No one else had rung any bell?"

"The butler is certain they did not—that his master had no visitors of any sort. The telephone is controlled by a switchboard in a cloak-room in the hall with a connecting line to the wall in the hall outside the butler's pantry. He is positive it did not ring during the evening."

"You interest me."

"When he heard the summons the butler took a tray which he had ready and proceeded to the library. This tray contained a carafe of whisky, a syphon of soda and a box of cigarettes and some biscuits for Coppot followed the 'night-cap' habit of your country, mon ami."

"And a point in his favour," murmured Blake.

But Thibaud, who hated whisky, made a grimace.

"The butler knocked on the door, but got no answer. Believing his master to be busy he tried the handle. It turned, and the door yielded, which showed that his master had unlocked it before ringing. He entered and then almost dropped his tray as he saw Coppot had fallen from his chair on to the floor. The butler laid the tray on the desk and bent over his master. It was then he saw a hole in the right temple and a nasty mess of the skull; also he spied a small automatic pistol lying on the floor, not far from the body, just as if it had dropped from Coppot's hand as he fell. He at once rang up the police, and, as you know, the inquest ended in a verdict of suicide. Of course, the affairs of Coppot's bank came under immediate scrutiny and, voila!—the crash in which poor, simple Emile Thibaud was caught."

"If it is all as you say, then why do you suspect foul play?" asked Blake in a puzzled tone.

Thibaud's face was utterly bland and simple in expression as he opened a drawer and took out a rather thick dossier enclosed in a green holder. He pushed this across to Blake, who read the pointed characters, stating whose dossier it was.

"Jules Cravette," he read; then he shot a look at Thibaud.

"Cravette—Cravette—that name is familiar to me, Thibaud. Let me remember— Paris, London, no, Marseilles—what was it. Why, I've got it now, he was mixed up in that old Rif business with the English renegade criminal, George Marsden Plummer. What has his dossier to do with Coppot's death?"

Thibaud chuckled.

"Cravette was the butler," he answered slyly.

CHAPTER 5. "Black Armand" Acts.

"JULES CRAVETTE!"

Sexton Blake leaned forward swiftly and opened the dossier. Thibaud lit a fresh caporal cigarette and, relaxing, watched Blake with an expression of mild amusement in his eyes.

Page after page he turned, scanning rapidly a phrase here, a paragraph there, until he came to the more recent particulars covering the known movements of Jules Cravette. Then, suddenly, he reached the last page and recognised the handwriting. It was Tinker's. It was then Blake remembered how he had dictated certain details to the lad just after his encounter with Plummer in Marseilles, this sheet regarding Cravette being sent as a matter of courtesy to the Surete where, naturally, it had gone into Thibaud's ready hands.

Blake noted the date, which was the last item Tinker had jotted down; then he looked up at Thibaud.

"Is this the last entry?"

"Alas, yes, mon ami! It is an unfortunate thing to confess, but until I saw the good Cravette in the rôle of butler at the house in the Avenue Marceau, I have not known his movements. But now a fresh page is in preparation."

"So it is because of Cravette that you are suspicious as to how Coppot died."

"That—and something else. Regardez, monsieur."

With that he opened another drawer and took out a small automatic pistol.

"You are expert in such weapons; tell me, please, if you note anything about this to remark."

Sexton Blake took the pistol and, rising, carried it to the window, from which he could see the blunt towers of Notre Dame and the lovely Pointed Tower which rises from the central dome of the great cathedral. Little did he dream as he bent to scrutinise the weapon that the slim fingers of Vali Mata-Vali had touched it only two nights before.

He examined the outer surface first; then he slid out the clip, laid it aside, and sprang the slide of the breech. Readjusting it he turned his head in Thibaud's direction.

"This is the weapon that was found on the floor?"

"Yes."

"I notice that the clip has a capacity of nine and one in the breech. But there are only eight in the clip. The barrel is powder-stained. You mentioned one wound only; was the cartridge-case found?"

"Yes; I have it."

"Then the pistol was fully loaded."

"That is the inference."

"It has been examined for finger-prints?"

"Yes. There was nothing clear enough to aid us."

"Um! Yet you expect me to make some discovery? Let me make a further examination."

Once more Blake held the pistol close to the window in order to get the full benefit of the light. He sought further assistance by taking a powerful pocket-glass from his waistcoat-pocket, and now he made a minute study of every inch of the dull, blued steel. At last he held the glass motionless, and, had he swung round quickly, he would have seen that Thibaud had an expression of almost childish delight on his broad countenance. At last Blake lifted his head, returned the glass to his pocket, and walked to his chair by the desk. He laid the pistol on the blotting-pad in front of Thibaud.

"What has become of the silencer?" he asked quietly.

The Frenchman chuckled outright.

"Oho! So you found the marks, my friend!"

"I should say that an easily adjustable silencer had been affixed to the end of the barrel at some time or other. It might be of the Fernet type, which, as you are well aware, can be bought at any gun shop in Paris."

"Aha! But we found no silencer with the pistol."

"You told me that Cravette answered the bell immediately after Coppot rang."

"That was his evidence."

"But Cravette may have been lying."

"That occurred to me," responded Thibaud plaintively.

"Then that washes out his tale that Coppot must have shot himself during the few minutes Cravette was occupied in bringing the tray from the butler's pantry to the library. On the other hand, if it were true that Coppot had had the library door locked all the evening, if he rose, unlocked the door, rang, and then returned to his seat at the desk, it would have been possible for him to lift the weapon, shoot himself, and fall as he was found without Cravette hearing the sound of the shot, even a short distance down the hall, if the pistol was fitted with a silencer."

"Quite sound."

" In that case, who removed the silencer from the pistol?"

"Aha!"

"I know you have canvassed all this in your own mind. By the way, what of the doctor's evidence?"

"It confirmed what Cravette said. He was on the scene about half an hour after death must have occurred, for he is quite positive that Coppot must have died about the time stated by Cravette!"

"Then what about that silencer, if it was on the pistol when the shot was fired?"

"Cravette," murmured Thibaud.

"Is it your theory that Cravette knew Coppot had a large sum in cash and negotiable securities with him that night— that he suspected Coppot's intention to clear out—and that he did the killing and has hidden the loot?"

"I have not gone so far as that, but Cravette is Cravette. I am interested in him."

"Well, I'll tell you something, Thibaud —Cravette never pulled off that stunt alone. He is not a leader; he could not plan a major crime. He was the tool of someone else. Cravette is not the man to make a play for millions. He is a killer— yes, but only when he acts under the orders of someone else."

But Blake did not add what was in his own mind, since remembering that Jules Cravette had been one of Plummer's gang at the time he had been up against the master-criminal in Marseilles.

"Would you like to visit the place?"

"Before I return, yes. What else was found?"

"Two bags packed with some clothing and personal belongings. There was not enough to provide a man for a long journey, but it was only later I had the talk with Coppot's fiancée and learned also about the yacht that was in waiting at Bordeaux. There was also the big black leather bag which was recognised by two persons as that which Coppot brought away from the bank that night. It was quite empty."

"No money, no securities at all were found?"

"Less than, a thousand francs in one of the drawers in the desk."

"Was there a safe?"

"There was—empty."

Blake glanced, at his watch and rose.

"I must return to my hotel now, Thibaud, for I promised to meet my principal, Mr. Bridges. But I should like to see the house in the Avenue Marceau. Do you think one could learn any more by a further interrogation of Coppot's fiancée?"

"I do not think she can tell us more."

"Of course it is impossible to see the body."

"Unless it is disinterred; he was buried immediately after the inquest in Pere Lachaise cemetery."

When Blake got back to the Carlitz he found Mr. Bridges in the lounge. Even before Blake reached him he could see that the banker was labouring under suppressed excitement. He took Blake by the arm and led him to a secluded corner.

"That scoundrel, Blake, there isn't a hope of our getting a penny out of the crash. But I've got something to tell you."

"What is it?"

"I was just leaving the bank when I was accosted by a young fellow who said he had been working in Coppot's bank. He offered me certain information at a price."

"You paid it?"

"I took him to a cafe and paid him one thousand francs to hear what he had to say."

"I wonder if I could guess what it was."

"What do you mean?"

"Was it that Coppot had been gathering together a large sum in securities over a considerable period, and that, on the last day he was alive he left the bank carrying a big black bag which this youth believes was stuffed with further loot?"

The banker's jaw dropped as he stared in amazement at the detective.

"Hang it, that is just what he did tell me. Have you seen him?"

"No, but one of the inspectors from the Surete has already interviewed him. It looks as though that young fellow was making as much as he could out of the affair. Did he tell you anything else?"

"Not of any importance. Have you discovered something?"

"One or two things. It seems likely that Coppot did have a big bunch of loot for his projected getaway, and there are reasons for suspecting that he did not die by his own hand. That, however, is in the strictest confidence. There is nothing to show that he had been speculating heavily on the Bourse; only a few trifling transactions can be traced to him. There is reason to believe that he took home with him a considerable sum in cash and securities that night, and it seems credible that he had other large amounts secreted. If that is so then why did he commit suicide? I cannot go any further than that, Mr. Bridges, but if he did not commit suicide —if the greater part of the embezzled funds were still intact, then they may still be in existence. This is all only a theory, but it has the support of the shrewdest detective of the Paris Surete, and it is my hope that I may learn their hiding-place before they have become separated and disbursed."

The banker plied him for further details, but Blake would not commit himself. After they had lunched, however, he did send off a note to Thibaud which ran as follows:

"If still convenient for you, could we go to the Avenue Marceau this afternoon about three? May I suggest that you send one of your men to bring in the youth who worked in Coppot's, bank for a further interrogation. He has been talking to others besides the police."

He despatched this by a special messenger, and within half an hour the boy was back with Thibaud's assurance that he would call for Blake at three o'clock. Thibaud added a postscriptum to the effect that he had sent a man to locate and bring in the youth Blake had mentioned.

That young man was not destined, however, to fall into the hands of the police. Within a few minutes of the English banker leaving him at the corner of the Rue Richelieu, a slim, dandified young man had sidled up to him, and, speaking in the apache manner out of one corner of his mouth had said:

"There is no need of a word between us. Get into this taxi."

The ex-bank clerk gave a look of sudden fear at his companion, for he had believed himself finished with this suave apache who had fed him small bribes in return for what he could tell him about Etienne Coppot. If he had known that the apache was known in the sinister Belleville district as "Black Armand," he would have been even more terrified, for, despite his spying work, and his willingness to sell information to Bridges as soon as he knew that individual had come across from London on behalf of the English banking firm who had acted as Coppot's London agents, he was not evil at heart.

His was simply a case of a youth living beyond his earnings, of a weak nature tempted by easy money. If he had guessed into what a terrible net he had been swept he would have fled from Paris to the uttermost limits of the world.

He summoned a sickly smile, and endeavoured to carry off his inward fear with an air of bravado.

"Oh! It is you," he said jerkily. "I haven't seen you for two days since—since—"

"Shut your mouth."

Armand's lips did not move the veriest trifle, but the words shot from the corner of his mouth with appalling viciousness. The next moment he hailed a taxi, and had the youngor fellow known of the wheels within wheels on which Armand's actions revolved, he would have realised that the driver must be in the confidence of the apache. As a matter of fact it was the man known as "Jean" who had driven the big limousine on the night that Etienne Coppot met his death.

Not a word was spoken all the way to the Belleville district. Armand sat close to his charge, his hard eyes glittering like bits of glass. Only once did he turn and look at his companion, a swift look that was accompanied by a quick snarl that made the youth shiver.

Once in that district of the lost, the cab took turning after turning until it reached a narrow, cobbled street out of which it would have to reverse if there should be no opening at the far end. Here it, stopped before an evil looking cafe.

"Out," ordered the apache.

"But what do you wish with me?" begged the other in trembling tones.

For answer the apache jerked out a knife and jammed the point through the other's coat until it was pricking his bare ribs.

"Out!"

He hesitated no longer. Painfully he stepped to the pavement, but if he had any idea of making a dash for freedom it was frustrated by Armand's hand which clutched him sharply.

"Walk!"

Together they entered the cafe, passing a zinc-topped bar behind which a huge, villainous-looking fellow was reading a dirty news-sheet. Armand guided his charge through a pair of half-swing doors into a gloomy room at the back where half a dozen men and women were drinking to the accompaniment of low whispered talk. Not a single glance was bestowed on the two as they passed.

At the back of this den was another door which gave into a short, dark hall. At the end of the hall was a staircase up which Armand forced his prisoner to precede him. But at the top he again clutched his arm, and then, with an oath, flung him into a room on the right. Out of the darkness came a whisper.

"Have you brought him?"

"Oui, monsieur."

"Then make haste."

The poor youth never knew just what happened. One moment he was standing in that dark room shaking from head to foot in deadly fear; the next, Armand's knife was buried to the hilt between his shoulder blades. He fell sideways, coughed just once, then lay still.

Armand straightened up. Had his fare been visible, one might have seen that his eyes were glassier than ever—the glitter of the killer. And thus he died, for, just as he had struck from behind, so did a blade come plunging at him to sink its greedy length into his black heart.

Once more a whisper came out of the darkness.

"Is it done, Pierre?"

"Oui, monsieur."

"You know what you have next to do."

"Oui, monsieur."

Suddenly a flashlight shone. Its beams lay on the prone form of Armand, the apache, which sprawled motionless across the body of his victim. The vague outline of a hand could be distinguished behind the light as it reached towards the shadowy bulk of a man who stood just where he had been when he struck down Armand. For a second the light fell on his face revealing the low brow and coarse features of Pierre.

"Hold the light, Pierre."

He reached out and grasped the barrel of the torch. Then he shifted it a little and held it so, while the other man bent over Armand and thrust something into a pocket; a few moments more sufficed to "plant" another object in the garments of the ex-bank clerk. Then he rose, and the light passed for the briefest space of time across the broad countenance of Emile Thibaud of the Paris-Surete.

CHAPTER 7.   Thibaud Springs a Surprise.

M. THIBAUD was prompt to keep his appointment with Sexton Blake. It was just three o'clock when an inconspicuous police car drew up in front of the Carlitz Hotel in the Rue de Rivoli.

Blake joined him at once, and the car started up the Champs Elysees. Just after they passed Claridges Hotel the man from the Surete pointed out a large block of flats, one of those luxuriously fitted buildings which have appeared in the Champs Elysees since the war.

"That is 87bis," he said, "the residence of Coppot's fiancée."

Blake gazed at the place with interest. On the third floor he could see that all the curtains were drawn.

"Is that her flat?"

"Yes."

"Have you examined it since she went to Enghien?"

Thibaud admitted that he had not neglected this precaution, adding that nothing of a nature to incriminate either the woman or Coppot had been found.

"What was your impression, Thibaud? Do you think she knew what he was up to?"

"I do not. She struck me as innocent, and there is no doubt she was taking his death hard. I have had her bank account traced. It appears that Coppot would not allow her to keep it in his bank—whether through caution or because he wished to protect her I cannot say. But the account is no more than a woman in her position would have; I gather that Coppot had settled fairly large amounts on her at different times."

They said no more until the car drew up in front of a splendid mansion in the Avenue Marceau. Its grilled outer doors were closed, but when Thibaud had rung Blake could see the inner vestibule doors open and a man appear who, he knew at first glance, was a plain-clothes man from the Surete.

"So you are still in charge," he murmured,

"While the good Cravette is here," rejoined Thibaud.

They passed through the vestibule into the hall. When the constable had closed the doors, Thibaud turned to him, saying curtly:

"The butler—summon him."

The man gazed at his superior in amazement.

"The butler—Cravette, monsieur? But monsieur himself took him away not half an hour ago. He has not returned."

The bland expression was no longer to be seen on Thibaud's face. His eyes were stern as Sexton Blake had seen them occasionally in the past.

"Fool! What are you talking about? I have not been near this house since yesterday."

The constable gazed at him helplessly, then turned his eyes on Blake.

"Explain yourself!" rasped Thibaud. "Ten thousand pink-eyed devils! What do you mean?"

"Monsieur, it is as I say," faltered the other. "Cravette went away with monsieur himself not half an hour ago."

Thibaud's shoulders almost touched his ears. He raised his hands to high Heaven.

"Pig of an imbecile!" he roared. "Dare you throw the lie in the teeth of Thibaud?"

Blake laid a hand on his arm.

"Wait, my friend," he said quietly. "The man is sincere. Get his story from him."

"You hear?" spluttered Thibaud. "The gentleman intercedes for you. Speak, imbecile!"

The constable made an effort to recover his poise. When he began to speak his voice was steadier and his words the formal ones so beloved of the police of all countries.

"Monsieur, I was on duty as usual when the bell rang. I went to the vestibule and saw monsieur outside with a large limousine waiting at the kerb. I opened the doors and permitted the entry of monsieur. Monsieur at once demanded the presence of the butler, Jules Cravette. I summoned the man and was instructed by monsieur to return to my place outside the door of the library. Monsieur spoke some words to Cravette which I could not distinguish; the monsieur seemed to grow angry, and I heard him say: 'Get you hat, and come with me. We will see if we can make you talk at the Surete.' Cravette obeyed, and since the orders were given direct by monsieur I could do nothing but permit him to go."

"That is all?" asked Thibaud, who was again calm.

"Oui, monsieur."

Thibaud turned to Blake.

"What think you of that, my friend?"

"I should say that someone had cleverly impersonated you, Thibaud, and had spirited Cravette away."

Thibaud swung back to the constable.

"You did not suspect that it was not I?"

"No, monsieur. If it was not monsieur it was sufficiently like to be monsieur's twin brother."

"And you say this happened half an hour ago?"

"Just before a quarter to three, monsieur."

"Unlock the door of the library. I telephone to the Surete."

Thibaud got through to M. Dupuis. No one else would do in such an astonishing contretemps as this. Never in all his years at the Surete had Emile Thibaud been up against such a bare-faced move on the part of any criminal; for now he was in full agreement with what Sexton Blake had suggested.

The prefect promised to send out a general alarm at once, and advised Thibaud to return to headquarters as soon as possible. Thibaud assured him he would do so, but that first he wished to show Blake over the mansion.

They began their examination in the library. The man from the Surete showed Blake just where Coppot's body had been found, and the spot, still roughly chalked, where the pistol had been lying. Next they went into the adjoining room where the bags had been found partially packed, as if Coppot had been getting them ready for his flight. He opened the safe to show Blake its empty interior; then they proceeded to make a tour of the whole building from garret to cellars.

Yet, though he used his eyes every instant, Blake failed to hit upon anything in the nature of a clue. Every window and door had already been tested for signs that a forced entry had been made, but no such marks had been found.

By the time they were back in the lower hall Blake had to agree that if Thibaud's suspicions were correct—if Coppot had been murdered and the loot stolen, then suspicion pointed strongly to Jules Cravette as having been concerned in the crime. And there was the amazing impersonation of Thibaud which had taken place only about half an hour before their arrival on the scene.

That alone was sufficient to indicate a daring and resourceful brain behind the affair. Nor could Blake get out of his mind the recollection that Cravette had been associated with George Marsden Plummer. Plummer was quite clever and daring enough to pull off such a murder and to nip Cravette out from under the very noses of the police once he knew who was in charge of the case; for Blake did not doubt that Plummer would possess an espionage service that would keep him informed of Thibaud's every movement.

But, according to Tinker, Plummer was in Slough, and not even the master-criminal could be in two places at the same time. More and more Blake had to confess that he was wandering in a maze at every turn of which he found some sign that George Marsden Plummer had been before him, but what lay in the heart of the maze was obscured by the twists and turns which had been cunningly contrived.

Thibaud dropped Blake at his hotel just before five o'clock. Bridges was in the lounge, ready to inform Blake what had taken place at the bank during the afternoon. No further resources had been discovered, and investigations had advanced far enough for the official auditors to announce that they did not expect to come upon any further cash or securities. What had been found at the central bank, and what could be collected at the various country branches would, as anticipated, scarcely pay the wages of the staff.

"So I don't see any use in remaining in Paris longer," he wound up gloomily. "It looks as if my firm would have to shoulder the total liabilities against the paper that went through us—unless you can suggest something, Mr. Blake."

The detective shook his head regretfully.

"I can suggest nothing just now, Mr. Bridges. I am sorry that the debacle is as it is, but I gathered as much from the information I received at the Surete. I have already taken you into my confidence to a certain extent, and I shall proceed to work along those lines. There lies, in my opinion, the only chance of recovering anything from the wreck."

"Well, I hope you will keep us in mind; you may rest assured we shall be only too glad to pay our share of your expenses and fees if you recover anything. But what puzzles me is why that scoundrel Coppot blew his brains out on the eve of his intended getaway. He must have had a big bunch of loot still in his possession, because you have informed me you do not think much has been dispersed, and the auditors are of the same opinion."

Blake nodded, but did not grow any more communicative. He thought it as well that, for the present, the news of the disappearance of the butler, Cravette, should remain a secret between him and the officials of the Paris Surete.

Blake sent a note to Thibaud that evening telling him they were leaving for London from the Gare St. Lazare at ten the next morning. When he and Bridges walked towards the gates giving on to the platform he was not surprised to see Thibaud standing beside the ticket collector, but he was certainly not prepared for the news that Thibaud had to whisper to him just before the train pulled out.

"Two bodies found in the Seine early this morning," was what he began with. "Two bodies, my friend. One was found against a factory wall at Asnieres, and the other in the rushes of a small island off Poissy. We have identified both bodies— one was a young man who worked for a time in Coppot's bank, and the other a well-known and notorious apache known, as 'Black Armand' —a crook of the Belleville district who has given us a lot of trouble."

"A clerk who worked in Coppot's bank," murmured Blake thoughtfully. "Do you attach any importance to it, Thibaud?"

The man from the Surete did not reply at once. He turned and beckoned to the guard, who was about to wave his starting flag.

"Not yet," he ordered curtly. "I am from the Surete—I shall give you the sign." And because the railways in France are State-owned he was obeyed. "Look at this, Blake," he went on. He took out a folded, crumpled note, which, when Blake opened it out under cover of his coat, he saw to be of the value of ten thousand francs. "Ten thousand francs, my friend, in the pocket of an out-of-work. What think you of that?"

"Did it appear to be suicide?"

"Not at all. The youth had been stabbed in the back by one who knew the job, and the knife was still sticking out from between his ribs. That knife belonged to Black Armand!"

"The devil!"

"He was that. Let us say that Black Armand killed the young fellow; then who killed Black Armand?"

"Ah! So he was murdered, too?"

"In the same way, and by the same means, but we have not yet been able to trace the owner of the knife. That of Black Armand had his initials cut on the handle, and many notches to count his victims. We knew all about that knife; Black Armand was proud of his killings, and boasted much among his friends of the underworld."

"Someone may have planted the ten thousand franc note in the other fellow's pocket for a purpose."

Thibaud smiled slightly.

"The note bears one of the serial numbers of a certain issue that is missing from the Coppot bank," he remarked, watching for what effect this startling statement would have on Sexton Bloke. Nor was he disappointed, for the English detective gave a low whistle.

"I almost wish I were remaining in Paris," he muttered. "You might have something else of interest to tell me."

Thibaud chuckled delightedly. He was in his element when he could get a rise, so to say, out of the imperturbable Blake.

"Aha! What would you say if I showed you something else before that impatient cabbage of a guard starts the train—something that was found in Black Armand's pocket!"

Blake gazed at him whimsically while he thrust a hand into an inside pocket.

"Spring it, Thibaud," he said pleasantly.

"Regardez-vous, monsieur. What think you of this?"

As he spoke he opened the fingers of his hand, disclosing, in the palm, a small silencer of the exact type and make which Blake had said might fit the automatic pistol which was found on the floor beside Coppot's body.

"The silencer!" he whispered. "In Black Armand's pocket?"

"Yes, my friend. And it fits perfectly. See—this clip? It touches the barrel just where you detected that mark. Oho! Thibaud, poor, simple Thibaud is not so slow. I think,"

"Anything else in your bag of wonders?" asked Blake good-humouredly. "If there is, I think, after all, I had better stay."

But Thibaud shook his head.

"That is all just now, my friend. But rest assured that Thibaud will keep in touch with you. And you will inform me if you discover anything in your country?"

"Of a surety."

And with his promise Blake shook hands, for the guard was growing more and more impatient.

Naturally Bridges was curious to know what the man from the Surete had had to say to Blake, but he found his companion entirely uncommunicative.

As a matter of fact, Blake had swept into fresh confusion the different pieces of the puzzle, and was making an entirely fresh attempt to refit them so as to get some coherent idea of the picture that would be formed when the jig-saw was complete.

Yet he did not discard his original theory that, although different methods had been employed to perpetrate the long series of swindles and crimes, there was a single mind behind them.

Until Peter J. Mendley had come to him he had entertained only an academic interest in the different coups. Naturally, he had followed what the papers had to say, and, in the intervals of his own cases, had voiced more than one opinion to Tinker that, while different methods might be employed, there were two things they shared in common.

One was the extraordinary daring that was employed; the other the magnitude of almost each crime. Yet it was not until Mendley asked him to undertake the rather prosaic-appearing investigation of the price of the new Marsden bicycle that he had entered the arena.

There was nothing at that time to tell him there could be any possible connection between a price cut in bicycles and a robbery in the Rue de la Paix—between a commercial incident in England and the daring swindle of a bank in Brussels.

It was Tinker really who had given him the connecting link, for it was the lad who had discovered George Marsden Plummer to be the head of the Marsden Cycle Co. The Marsden Cycle Co. and Plummer; it had begun there. Then the amazing swindle at the Haymarket branch of the Paris and Calais Bank, with suspicion linking up the perpetrators with Paris, and a definite connection between that affair and the fraud that had been practised on the bank in Brussels.

There were other robberies and swindles that had been listed in France, Belgium and Germany; there had been suspicious affairs in Vienna. No definite connection yet, it is true, but strong possibility that the same directing brain was behind them. Then the gigantic crash of the Coppot Bank in France, with the presumed suicide of Etienne Coppot.

But if Thibaud had been right—what then? If Blake's surmise that the automatic pistol found in Coppot's library had recently been fitted with a silencer was correct, was it murder? What of Cravette? Jules Cravette—Plummer! Plummer again! And the astounding daring with which Cravette had been spirited away from the mansion in the Avenue Marceau—who had impersonated Thibaud? Who had known his movements so well as to anticipate his visit to the house that afternoon? Who had guessed that Thibaud suspected murder and did not accept the theory of suicide?

For whom would most danger lurk if Cravette's dossier should come into question? George Marsden Plummer. And who was quite capable of carrying out the impersonation? Plummer. But if Tinker's report was correct, then Plummer must be at Slough. Blake shook his head, and, changing his line of analysis, dwelt on the finding of the two bodies in the Seine.

Two bodies—two murders. Was there any connection? It seemed there must be, for the ex-bank clerk had been killed with Black Armand's knife. If the apache had murdered the other, then who had killed him in turn? Then, another link—the ten-thousand-franc note that had been found in the pocket of the ex-bank clerk. Yet still another—the silencer in the pocket of the apache. Coppot—Plummer; Coppot— the ex-clerk; the ex-clerk—Black Armand; Black Armand—the silencer; the silencer— the pistol; the pistol—Coppot; Coppot— Plummer.

The circle was complete.

No matter which way one juggled the items it came to the same thing—Coppot— Plummer. And yet for the "nth" time Blake came up against what Tinker had said—Plummer was in Slough. It could not have been Plummer who had impersonated Thibaud unless he had made a sudden dash to Paris.

And that dash must have been after Coppot's death. If this were so, then someone else had been responsible for the actual carrying out of the crime at the mansion in the Avenue Marceau. Who was Plummer's most trusted partner? Whom would he trust to act in such a responsible rôle? Only one person had his complete trust— Vali Mata-Vali. And she was perfectly capable of directing such an affair. Coppot —Plummer; Plummer—Vali Mata-Vali. Could it be so?

From this point the detective threw his mind back to the original cause of his participation in the investigation. Peter J. Mendley and his anxiety over the price at which the Marsden bicycle was being sold. What interest had George Marsden Plummer in the legitimate manufacture and sale of bicycles?

Not for a moment did Blake believe that Plummer was conducting a business that showed a small profit on each machine. It was like nothing he knew of the master-criminal's character. If it was Plummer who had directed and was still directing the crimes and swindles which seemed to form part of the same series, then what cog was that bicycle factory in the scheme of things?

Where was the most puzzling problem of all? Not the actual robberies and frauds. Where did the cloud obscure the affair most? The puzzle of the disposal of the loot! True, some of the stolen notes and securities had found their way into circulation—but that was because the thieves had needed the "sinews of war," as Inspector Thomas had put it.

But the jewels—what had become of that huge haul from the establishment in the Rue de la Paix? How had Plummer, if he were the head of the gang, tackled this difficulty? Was there any connection between that and the bicycle factory at Slough? Was the factory but a blind for something else?

The more and more he dwelt on this question, the more Blake became convinced that in sending Tinker to Slough in the first place he had, all unwittingly, made the exact move which should have been made. And long before he reached Baker Street that night he was anxious to got in touch with the lad and learn what further he had to report.

Unfortunately, Blake was to hear nothing from Tinker that night. Had he not been in Paris when Tinker 'phoned he would have learned that Plummer had not been seen for two days. All he did find was a brief note from Tinker saying he was sorry he had missed Blake on the 'phone, and reporting that for a full day he had seen no signs of Plummer.

He mentioned having discovered the house where Plummer was living and named it Marsden Manor; he also gave a brief resume of the goods that had been received at the factory during the past few days and one of shipments of finished bicycles going out.

On the face of it one could not but concede that a large and genuine business was being done. Yet, despite the honest appearance of the particulars, Sexton Blake gave the items a strict analysis before going to bed.

The result of this was that he jotted down one or two notes, to which he intended giving more detailed attention the following morning. The first was Tinker's item stating that five thousand steel frames had been received from Sheffield; the second was that a shipment of frames, twelve thousand in number, had been received from a shipper in France; still a third was that he had noticed, in the receiving warehouse, crates marked with the names of shippers in

Brussels, Dijon (France), Nancy (France) and Marseilles.

Sexton Blake tapped those pencilled notes very thoughtfully.

"Sheffield," he muttered. "Is it possible there is any connection? The cashier of the steel mills in Sheffield was killed and some nine thousand pounds in wages stolen. Now, here again—Brussels; that recalls the swindle worked by means of the forged Spanish letter of credit. Umm! Why the dickens should the Marsden Cycle Co. buy their frames from so many different sources? I am not a manufacturer of bicycles, but it seems to me that if I wished to make certain of a standardised model I would endeavour to contract for all my frames from one manufacturer, all my handlebars from another, all my bearings from another, and so on. But the Marsden Cycle Co. seem to jump all over the place for their various parts. How can a French manufacturer turn out a frame similar to this factory in Sheffield, for example? And here again, Tinker finds shipments of frames from places as far apart as Nancy, Dijon and Marseilles. And in the first two cities, at any rate, there have been robberies which I have already suspected as being part of the series which I have linked together. Sheffield, Brussels, Nancy, Dijon—bicycle frames. What does it mean? What can it mean? Where does it all come within the circumference of the circle? And what bearing, if any, can it have on the Coppot Bank smash?

He gave it up then, and, after a final pipe, turned in. He was tired after his journey, and the mental concentration of several hours past, so he fell asleep almost at once; but even at that he would not have closed his eyes had he guessed what Tinker was heading for at that same hour.

CHAPTER 8.   Tinker In Trouble.

TINKER did not waste much time being peevish over Blake's sudden journey to Paris. He was naturally a self-reliant youngster, and Blake had trained him too carefully and thoroughly for the lad to need any "spoonfeeding." He had been sent to Slough on a job, and he would handle it to the best of his ability. If Blake wasn't in London to receive his reports over the telephone, he would send informal written advices and carry on his own initiative.

When a second day had passed without Plummer showing up at the factory, Tinker began to get a little anxious. One way and another he managed to keep a close eye on the receiving warehouse, the shipping rooms and the offices, but closing-down time came without Plummer putting in an appearance.

When he passed through the gates with the rest of the workmen, Tinker told himself that he would go straight to his boarding-house, get cleaned up, have his supper, and then try again to get through to Blake on the telephone. But when he had finished his meal he decided to lose no time in trying to get a line on Plummer's movements.

"I can write later, and the guv'nor will get the letter in the morning," he told himself. "Anyway," he added as an afterthought, "he may still be in Paris." Up in his room he made a few changes in his appearance and took care to stuff an automatic in his pocket, as well as a small jemmy and a flashlight. He read until dusk had definitely settled in, then, turning out the light, he made his way downstairs. As he passed the door of the common-room a young follow who had chummed up with him called out to ask him to walk down the road and play a game of billiards. Tinker put him off pleasantly and got away; then he turned his steps purposefully towards the western end of the town, where he would pick up the main road that ran past Marsden Manor and on up the Thames Valley to Maidenhead and beyond.

He knew his way, for the previous evening he had done a little scouting. He had got as far as the high wall that bounded the Manor, and had seen enough to realise that the grounds were very extensive as well as heavily timbered. He had learned these and other trivial facts from the gossip who had told him that the boss of the works lived there. But what he might find beyond that great enclosing wall he could not guess.

There was no moon, but the stars were out, and a faint twinge of grey still lingered along the western horizon, giving quite enough light for him to distinguish the road. He kept well to one side of the road, for there was a good deal of motor traffic running in both directions. All the time, however, he kept his eyes to the left, watching for the first signs of the wall which was his landmark. On the right was nothing but the flat ground between the road and the railway where the great factories lay sleeping, vast grey hulks gloomy and stark.

It was the brilliant lights of an overtaking car that first showed him his objective, looming about fifty yards ahead. As soon as the car was past he climbed over the fence and took his way along a rough field that before long would be occupied by rows of cottages for workpeople. But now they formed a desolate belt about the great wall bounding the Manor, washing right up against it, as it were.

Tinker kept on until he was in under the shadow of the brick. He knew that a pair of heavy wrought-iron gates gave entrance at the front, but on his previous expedition he had been unable to see any other means of entry on either side. What lay at the back he did not know yet, but he intended finding out within the next few minutes.

Using the wall as his guide, he crept along until he reached the far corner. Judging the distance from the road as well as possible, he reckoned he had come a good quarter of a mile, and, on his first visit, he had calculated the front to extend fully that distance. A quarter of a mile square meant very extensive grounds and complete seclusion for the occupant of the Manor.

Now he swung the corner to the right and pressed along, feeling constantly for some signs of a break on the straight surface of the brick. With a ladder it would not have been difficult to get over the top, despite the double row of sharpened spikes which he had seen there; but without such means of assistance he knew it was out of the question to climb the twelve feet that rose sheer above him.

It was not the first, time, however, that Tinker had tackled a problem of that sort. In fact, so confident was he that he would be on the other side of that wall within a few minutes, he sniffed at it in disdain.

"Think you're as good as a gaol, I suppose," he muttered. "Well, we'll see, old bricks and mortar."

It was just as this moment that his hand suddenly left the bricks and encountered nothingness; then, as he pushed his arm forward he felt smooth wood. It was a door in the wall, but it was too dark for him to make out its size or what possibilities it had of being opened.

His exploring fingers came at last to a large keyhole, and, just beneath that, an iron handle guard inside which was a latch. He tested the latch and pressed, without any hope that the door would yield so he was not disappointed when it refused to budge.

He straightened up and listened. Some distance away he could hear the rumble of a train, and, beyond the front wall, the hoot of motor-horns on the main road. But near at hand nothing reached his ears. He had been unable to see the Manor that lay within the walls, and therefore had no idea whether it was tenanted on this night or empty.

Satisfied that he had no immediate cause for alarm, he bent once more, and this time he brought his electric flash into play. He soon assured himself that the lock, though large and suitable for its purpose, was not beyond his powers, so taking out the bunch of skeleton keys he always carried he chose the largest.

No luck with this one nor with the next. The keyhole was deceptive, he thought, or else he needed a skeleton larger even than his largest. Still he persisted, this time employing the third in size, and a few minutes later he uttered a grunt of satisfaction as he felt it turn in his hand. "Got you!"

Once more he tried the latch, and from the fact that the door eased inwards the barest fraction of an inch he knew that he had succeeded in pressing back the bolt; but still the door did not yield more than that insignificant trifle.

"Barred or bolted as well," he muttered in deep disappointment. "Nothing for it but to go over the top. Wonder if I can manage by using the latch guard as a foothold? Might be able to reach the top from there. Here goes, anyway."

He moved the flashlight up and down until he had covered the whole area of the door. He found it to be a massively-built affair evidently of some considerable age. It was single, made of three stout planks which were painted green; but he guessed the wood beneath the paint was oak. In height it was about six feet six, and in width about five feet. No other obstruction showed except the latch and the iron guard. Above the door frame the wall rose to the spiked top.

Tinker switched off the light and returned it to his pocket. Then he made effort after effort to get sufficient hold on the side of the door frame until he could support one foot on the top of the guard. But again and again he fell back, until he sank to the ground panting from his efforts.

So engrossed had he been in trying to overcome the barrier that confronted him that he was quite oblivious of any noise he might have made, but now caution reasserted itself, and he sat up to listen. Still nothing but those distant traffic sounds came to him.

At last he gathered himself together and approached the door once more. Bringing out his torch he switched it on, and once more began an examination of the lock. He tried to peer in the keyhole, but could see nothing. Next he took out his bunch or skeleton keys.

"Never can tell," he thought. "Maybe I didn't turn far enough. I'll have another shot at it, anyway, and if I don't shift it this time I'll scout round and see if I can find an empty box or something of the sort."

Selecting the skeleton key that had seemed before to work the oracle, he inserted it in the keyhole and began to twist and turn as before. When he felt the shaft go almost its full length he turned to the right, finding it stopped just at the angle of his first attempt.

He persisted more out of doggedness than anything else, and thought he managed to turn it the veriest trifle more, but could not be sure. It was more a mechanical attempt than anything else that made him try the latch once more and press his knee against the wood. Then he felt the heavy door move away from him, and could scarcely restrain a low whistle of amazement as it swung open more and more, allowing him to step over the timber threshold into the grounds on the other side.

He closed it carefully and stood peering ahead into the gloom. He could just make out the gleam of a light somewhere ahead through the thickly-dotted trees of the park-like grounds, and was about to move cautiously in that direction when, without the slightest warning, a pair of powerful arms gripped him from behind.

"Want to get in, do you?" snarled a voice in his ear. "All right, my prowling bucko; you won't be disappointed."

With that he was lifted into the air and smashed to the ground with such force that every breath was driven from his body, and every organ felt as if it must have been jolted out of position. Half unconscious from the shock, he was unable to make a single move to defend himself, and thus was forced to yield without a struggle when the same ruthless arms picked him up as if he were a feather and slung him across a shoulder. Next moment his captor was striding along at a pace that held sinister purpose in every step.

CHAPTER 9.   At the Marsden Works.

ONLY those workmen who were employed in the bearings fitting section of the Marsden works, and more particularly his bench mate, who had palled up with him, took any notice of the fact that young "Charles Turner" was not in his place the following morning —that is, they and the foreman of that section. It was not long past seven o'clock when the foreman came along and stood beside Bert Coggin, the young fellow in question.

"Where's Turner this morning?" he asked gruffly.

"I don't know; ain't seen him."

"You board at the same place, don't you?"

"Yes."

"And you usually come on the job together, because I've seen you."

"That's right, but I didn't see him this morning. I waited for him a few minutes after breakfast, but he didn't show up, so I thought he had gone on ahead."

"Did he get 'stewed' last night?"

"I've never seen him take a drink. He didn't strike me as that sort. But I didn't see him last night after he went out."

"Oh, he went out, did he?"

"A little while after supper."

"Huh! Well, if he doesn't turn up this afternoon you can tell him when you go home that he's fired. Got that?"

"Yes."

With that the foreman walked on to inspect the time clock while Coggin sent a look of dislike after him.

"Dirty rotter!" he muttered. "What does he want to pump me about Turner for? I wouldn't tell him anything even if I knew it. Just the same, I'd like to know where Charlie got to last night. I wish I'd gone to his room this morning. I've never seen him hit the booze, but maybe he binges now and then, and perhaps that's why he didn't want me along with him last night, him knowing I don't drink. Well, it's none of my funeral; let him look out for himself. I ain't going to worry."

All the same, he did worry off and on during the day, for he was a decent young fellow, and had taken a decided liking to "Charlie Turner." If he had but known what had happened to his pal!

The Marsden factory had been closed several hours that night when the head of the firm arrived in Slough. He was not seen by the few persons he passed, for the simple reason that he sat in a big saloon car with the blinds drawn. Nor could anyone guess that he had for company a very smartly-dressed young woman, who yawned sleepily now and again.

No one in Slough had yet been privileged to enter Marsden Manor although many had called, including the bishop and the vicar. Each visitor had been received by a pompous-looking butler, who had politely but firmly informed them that his master was "not at home." And since the people of Slough knew of no chatelaine, the ladies could scarcely be expected to take such a step until the actual fact of such a person was brought to their notice.

As the saloon car passed the road gates of the factory that housed the activities of the Marsden Cycle Co., the president and managing director, Mr. Gerald Marsden, lifted one of the blinds and touched his companion on the arm. He pointed to a huge electric sign that ran right across the front of the building, blazoning forth to all who passed that here was the home of Marsden Cycles. His companion roused herself and laughed softly.

"It would be droll, my dear boy, if you should unwittingly make legitimate money out of that playbox."

Plummer grinned.

"It's no joke, Vali, I can tell you. As a matter of fact, we are making a net profit at the moment of about two shillings on each machine, and I'll bet there isn't a set of books in the country that can stand up under a more rigorous examination than those of the Marsden Cycle Co. I didn't know it was so easy. I could raise the price of the machines by five shillings to-morrow and still undersell my competitors. I should never have believed that advertising could put a thing on the world's market as quickly as this bicycle has been placed. Why, my dear girl, it is world known already; we are shipping thousands of machines a week to cities and towns in the British Isles as well as to half a hundred points abroad. And the joke of the whole thing is that our buyers are getting a first-class article that our competitors can't touch. I bet some of them are doing some hard thinking right now."

She looked serious for a moment.

"Do you really mean you could make such a good thing out of it?"

"If I raised the price—sure."

"I wonder why you don't do so," she remarked curiously.

Plummer made a sound of impatience. "Me! I should worry. I'd go off my nut fooling round with a game of that sort. I may put in a competent man to manage it for me, and run it as a side line; but the other game for me, Vali, and for you, too, I guess. We've gone too far now to turn back."

She laughed lightly.

"You are right, old boy; it wouldn't do for storm birds like us. All the same, it seems a pity to let it go if it has such possibilities."

"I'm not going to let it die. I've got an idea that will put a couple of hundred thousand in our pockets in a perfectly legitimate way, and we'll pay dividends, too."

"What is the scheme?"

"A little later on when the Marsden bicycle is still more firmly established I'll float a public company and get the shares listed on the Stock Exchange. I'll do it, by heavens, if only to see one man squirm. And he won't be able to lift a finger, for it will be dead on the level. We'll take a nice bunch of common stock in consideration of our present holdings, goodwill, and so on, and then, my dear, we will unload when the price on 'change has gone to a premium. And I'll see that the same bird gets a few of them."

"Whom do you mean?"

"Sexton Blake."

She frowned at a sudden thought.

"You know he was in Paris yesterday?"

"I knew it—with Thibaud. I wouldn't be surprised if he was with Thibaud when that old fool got a shock at Coppot's house. Ha, ha! I'd have given a bunch of money to see their faces when they found that Cravette was missing."

She echoed his laugh, but again she spoke, in a warning note.

"He'll bear watching, George. He was over there in connection with the Coppot business, and you make a mistake in under-estimating Thibaud,"

"Don't you worry, my dear," rejoined Plummer confidently. "We've got this thing dead open and shut. They haven't got within a mile of us since we started. One or two more coups and get rid of the stuff. Then we finish—close up shop and sweep away every shred of evidence. I tell you it will be the biggest thing of its kind in a century.

You leave it to me, Vali. You and I will be rich—rich beyond our wildest dreams when we wind up this business. Then for a quiet life and— ha, ha, ha!—our dividends from the Marsden Cycle Co. And here we are at the gates of Marsden Manor, dear. Your first visit, so we must crack a bottle of fizz to drink your homecoming. I hope you will like it. Home and safety, Vali."

They swept through the big gates just then, and the precious pair gazed out through the windows—the blinds of which Plummer had thrown up—towards the bulk of the great mansion that loomed ahead. But the opening of that bottle of fizz was to be delayed, for there was an unpleasant surprise waiting for the master criminal.

Inspector Thomas would have recognised the pompous looking butler who opened the door as one "Jewey Dick." whose speciality in crime was rigging the inside for the "screw man." They had his photograph at Scotland Yard, both in profile and full face; and in that vast collection of fingerprints which is unrivalled, Jewey Dick's smudges were carefully preserved.

Inspector Thomas would have described the crook as the slickest man at his job that could be found. As a butler he was entirely admirable, and many a job had been worked through the efficient inside presence of Jewey Dick. He had done more than one stretch in prison, as well as two "journeys," but for some time past he had managed to leave a blank trail for the "Johns" and "flatties." At the present time he was as useful to Plummer at Marsden Manor as Cravette had been at Coppot's mansion in Paris.

Yet, even in the security of the Manor, he bowed as ceremoniously to Plummer and Vali Mata-Vali as if he were in sooth all that he appeared, and his master nothing but the prosperous head of the Marsden Cycle Co. It was the first time he had set eyes on Vali, but he gave no sign of his inward thoughts. He was telling himself, however, that now he understood why Plummer, who had always worked alone, had fallen for a "skirt."

Vali Mata-Vali gazed with true appreciation at the appointments of the great hall, at one end of which a cheerful log-fire was burning. It was just as its previous owners had left it, for Plummer had bought the place lock, stock, and barrel. When the butler had taken their things Plummer walked with Vali to one of the low easy-chairs that were drawn up in front of the fire.

"Sit down, my dear, and make yourself comfortable, while I

attend to things. I want to know what has taken place since I have been away. Richards"—this happened to be the name which "Jewey Dick " possessed when he entered this world, though few persons but himself knew it— "bring madame a cocktail; then call the maid. When you have done that, come to the study."

Jewey Dick bowed, and retired. Plummer looked with humorous eyes at Vali.

"You are wondering if Richards is safe," he said, as he drew out his cigar-case.

"Put your mind at ease, my dear; his better-known cognomen is Jewey Dick, and he has been behind the bars a dozen times. I can put him back there at a moment's notice."

She laughed and nodded.

"I needn't have had any doubts, but he looks so utterly respectable."

"That is his long suit," rejoined Plummer, with a grin. "Here he comes with your cocktail, Vali; and Anna, your maid, is coming down the stairs. I've got her as safe as I've got Richards, so go the limit. I'll rejoin you inside half an hour."

With a nod, the master-criminal turned, and, humming a little French song, made his way to a door on the right which gave into a small but very cosily furnished study. Such was the peculiar make-up of the man that he was as content and at ease in mind as if he were any honest business man back from a brief business trip, and glad again to find the comforts of his own fireside.

There were no letters in the ordinary sense on his desk; just a large blue linen envelope thickly stuffed with papers. He knew it contained certain reports, to which he would give attention later. Other correspondence he would find waiting for him at his business offices the next day.

He sat down at the desk and waited until Jewey Dick knocked at the door. Then, when the man entered and closed the door, Plummer looked up lazily.

"Well, Jewey Dick, any news?"

"I should say there is, chief," came the answer, in quick, smooth tones that one would never have associated with the precise, pompous accents of Richards, the butler.

George Marsdcn Plummer sat up quickly.

"What do you mean?"

"We've netted a bird while you've been away."

"When?"

"Last night."

"A 'flattie'?"

"Naw—a chicken."

"Where is he?"

"In the cellar."

"What the devil was he after?"

"I don't know. Jimmie has searched him, and found enough to identify him as one of the fellows at the works."

"One of the men at the factory, eh? What was it—plain burglary?"

"He won't talk. We've kept him for you. Come and give him the once over, chief."

Plummer's eyes were hard as marbles as he rose—those strange ember eyes that could glow with such an extraordinary light.

"I'll come, but—wait. Where did you pick him up?"

"He was trying to get in at the door in the back wall. He may be a 'screws' man, because we found a 'stick' on him as well as a 'flashy' and a pistol; also one of the factory cards with his name."

"What is it?"

"Charles Turner?"

"Did he put up a fight?"

"He didn't get a chance. He was making enough row to wake a dead man. Jimmie was on the prowl, and heard him— slipped the bar, and waited. Then he grabbed him."

"But how did he work the lock?"

"I forgot—he had a bunch of 'skillies.' "

"All right. Let's have a look at him." No longer did Plummer appear the contented business man. His jaw was set and thrust out aggressively as he flung open the door and stepped into the hall. But his voice was suave enough as he called to Vali:

"A little business to attend to, my dear; I shall not be long."

She nodded, but did not turn. Had she done so she would have recognised the signs that were flagged in Plummer's face. But she went on telling Anna, the maid, what she required of her, quite ignorant of the identity of the prisoner who lay gagged and bound in one of the cellars beneath her.

Plummer and Jewey Dick passed through three cellars before

they reached a small inner cellar, where a huge man sat in a big wooden armchair at one side of a heavy wooden door. He rose at sight of Plummer, but so tall was he that he had to bend his head to keep from banging it on the rafter above him.

"Well, Jimmie, I hear you netted a chicken?"

The man's answer came in the husky voice of the confirmed whisky drinker. "Yes, chief. Jewey has told you."

"Uhuh. Why couldn't you make him talk?"

"I could have squeezed all he ever knew out of him, chief, but Jewey and I, we thinks it best to wait until you came back, seeing as how he came from the works."

"All right, Jimmie, open the door and let's have a look at him."

Jimmie, an ex-burglar, took a big key from his pocket and thrust it into a gigantic keyhole. He turned, and then dragged the door open. The cellar inside was even smaller than the one in which they stood, but, like all the others, was well lighted by electric bulbs. They were well equipped and very dry, those cellars, but nothing like so amazing as others which Plummer was to visit before that night was over.

In this one was a small iron cot, a table, a chair, and a cupboard. It was as nearly like a cell as may be, with the exception that it had no bars by which daylight could enter, even had it not been night. On the bed lay the bound and gagged figure of a youth, and, at a sign from Plummer, Jimmie removed the gag. Then Plummer bent over the bed, studying the face that was upturned to his. For some minutes his amber eyes played over the features of the prisoner; then he smiled cruelly.

"So," he said, at last, and, at the metallic click in his voice, both Jewey Dick and Jimmie pricked up their ears, for that timbre was enough to tell them that more lay in this capture than they had suspected. "So," repeated Plummer, "it is you, you little fox!" Suddenly he swung round to Jewey Dick. "What did you say his name was on the card?"

"Turner—Charles Turner, chief."

"And he has been working at the factory, eh? Jimmie, you touch an extra 'pony' for bagging this chicken. Do you know who he is?"

The two crooks shook their heads. Plummer took one more look at the prisoner; then he laughed harshly.

"Then take a good look at him," he snarled, "because it is the whelp who acts as assistant to Sexton Blake."

CHAPTER 10.   The Crook of Marsden Manor.

ALTHOUGH free to speak during those minutes when Plummer gazed down upon him, Tinker made no attempt to do so. His mouth was ragged and sore from the brutal gag which Jimmie had jammed between his teeth, one of those vicious "pear" gags which expand to the full capacity of the jaw stretch, leaving them aching for hours after; but he could have articulated had he made the effort.

He kept mum, however. In fact, he had been so utterly chagrined since his capture the night before that he had fallen into a state of depression that he was in danger of all initiative becoming dulled until it might be too late even to make a fight for freedom, desperate though his chances might appear.

Both Jewey Dick and Jimmie had tried to make him speak each time they gave him food and water. They had not deprived him of those needs of the body, although the administration had been accompanied each time by dire threats of what would happen to him unless he told why he was trying to get into the Manor.

But Tinker gambled that they would not proceed to very stern measures until they should receive orders from Plummer, and, in addition, he soon saw that the discovery of the skeleton keys, the jemmy, the automatic and the flashlight, made them look upon him as an ordinary burglar. The works card which they also brought to light caused them to conclude that he had simply got a job there until he should have a chance to size up the crib he was going to crack.

If he hadn't done any talking, Tinker had done a good deal of bitter thinking. Over and over he kept reproaching himself—kept repeating that he had fallen down on the job. What would Blake say? He was on the 'phone when Tinker told him that the head of the Marsden Cycle Works was none other than George Marsden Plummer.

Blake had told him to carry on—had gone off to Paris evidently thoroughly satisfied that he (Tinker) was perfectly capable of handling matters in Slough until his return. And now this ignominious finish to all his fine plans.

Gall and wormwood it was to the high-spirited lad. He had been anxious at not having seen Plummer for two days, but had been confident that he would find some explanation at the Manor. Yet even after his capture a full twenty-four hours had gone by before Plummer put in an appearance.

He knew the period of time and that Plummer was away, for neither Jewey Dick nor Jimmie had been too guardful of their words in front of him, so safe did they feel about him. Perhaps they would have talked a little more cautiously had they guessed the importance of their capture. But to them he was just a burglar whom they had not before run up against—a person about whom they need fear nothing from the police.

Not even Blake could have been as scathing to the lad as Tinker was in his self-denunciation. And, during those few minutes when the discovery was made by Plummer that he knew must be inevitable, he held his peace, for something in the cruel glare of those amber eyes told him he was going to need all his strength and courage before Plummer finished with him.

He lay perfectly quiescent while, at a gesture from Plummer, the two other crooks again gagged him. He closed his eyes, but he was listening when Plummer said: "Move your chair inside, Jimmie. I wouldn't take a chance on this infernal young spy. He'll slide through the keyhole while you wink your lids. Watch him, and Heaven help you if he isn't here when I return, or I'll skin you alive. Come along, Jewey; I'll attend to his case after supper. I'll make him talk or I'll have his tongue out."

With that he gave a last threatening look at Tinker, but the lad did not see it, for he still kept his eyes closed. And glad he was now that he had held his peace during those twenty-four hours, for he knew that the moment was fast approaching when he would be face to face with the worst tiger among criminals. If he had known that the "tigress" was also close at hand he would have sunk into a deeper state of despair had it been possible.

Vali Mata-Vali needed only one quick glance at Plummer's face to realise that something serious had arisen. She was still sitting in one of the big easy-chairs talking to the maid, but after that swift look she dismissed Anna and waited while Plummer took up his stand before the blaze. He lit a cigarette, but waited until Anna had disappeared up the broad staircase.

"What is it?" she asked, in a low tone.

Briefly, Plummer told her of the unpleasant surprise that had awaited their return.

"It can't be accident," he went on thoughtfully. "And I haven't made any mistake."

"You are sure it is Blake's assistant?"

"Absolutely. I have seen that whelp too often in the past not to know him. But what game is Sexton Blake playing? He can't suspect the truth; I'll wager anything you like that not a soul has twigged that."

"Then why would he send his assistant as a workman to your factory?"

The master-criminal knit his brows in irritation.

"I'll find out before I finish with him," he premised grimly.

"You know Blake was with Thibaud in Paris."

"I know that; but he can't link up anything between the Coppot affair and the works here at Slough. I tell you, I know the scheme is safe. Anyone from the Commissioner at the Yard down can spend all the time they want at the works here, and they'll find nothing. But I'm puzzled just the same."

"Do you think Thibaud could have told him anything?"

"No. I have had a look at the brat's works card. It is made out in the name of 'Charles Turner,' and, from the date, I know he was employed by my production manager before Blake went to Paris. It isn't anything that happened in Paris; it is something that has come up on this side of the water."

"Well, there was the affair at the Paris and Calais Bank," she murmured. "At any rate, it isn't so serious now that you have him in your power. You didn't waste much time in dealing with Armand after he finished off the young bank clerk."

George Marsden Plummer was a criminal who had never been known to stop at any lengths to gain his ends. Killing came as part of the day's work, though he was usually too clever to do the actual job himself. It was his policy to employ tools to carry out his orders, for, aside from covering his own trail, it put the creatures in his power.

In Paris he had realised that his only means of killing the scent was to wipe out those who had played an active part in the Coppot affair about whom he had the least suspicion. It had come to his ears that the young bank clerk had been talking too much. If the police should get hold of him it wouldn't take them long to discover that he had been passing on information to "Black Armand."

Plummer did not trust the apache in a crisis any more than did Vali Mata-Vali. Only Plummer's cute mind could have evolved the simple yet diabolical scheme of fixing things so that Black Armand should knife the young fellow, and, even as he did so, to have him meet a like fate at the hands of Pierre.

Pierre and Jean were both to be trusted as was Cravette. He had dealt with them too often not to know every twist of their minds. But he never had felt sure of Armand, though the apache was the best person to employ for the special work he had performed in the Coppot affair. Then the masterly stroke of planting the ten-thousand-franc note in the pocket of the one and the pistol-silencer in the pocket of the other. No one but George Marsden Plummer would have anticipated that someone from the Surcte might suspect how Coppot had died, and might find the faint, tell-tale marks on the barrel of the automatic where the silencer had been affixed.

Therefore he took Vali's remark to be a perfectly ordinary part of the conversation. Nevertheless, well as he knew her, he could not resist sending her a quick look of admiration. Had he searched the wide world for a partner he could not have found one more suited to his tastes than she. She flinched from nothing; she did not seem to have a nerve in her whole make-up. She was the consort, par excellence, of one who had earned and gloried in the name "master-criminal."

But he shook his head,

"It would be easy enough to finish him off to-night, and no one would be the wiser. But I'm going to find out first what he was doing at the works. He must have spotted me, and from that found out about this house. He was out to get inside and discover something definite, Blake may or may not know what he learned. But Blake never sent him to the works without having some strong motive behind it. We've kept close tabs on what the police have been doing about things, and not once has Sexton Blake appeared until he turned up with Thibaud in the Avenue Marceau. A cog has slipped somewhere, and I've got to find out what it is."

"That shouldn't be very difficult," she murmured.

"You leave it to me, my dear," he rejoined grimly. "But first I must inspect what has been done in the other direction. This Coppot business has stirred up a bigger rumpus that I counted on. With Thibaud suspicious, you never know what will break. The only weak part that I can see is Cravette, and we have him safe here in England. Just the same, I want to get as much of the 'stuff' shipped away as we can, because there are several crates of bicycles ready to be sent abroad, and it is risky keeping too much on hand. Let's have something to eat first, then I'll see to matters."

When they had finished a very recherché supper in the big Tudor dining-room, Plummer suggested that Vali should go up to the rooms that had been prepared for her, promising to send Anna for her in case she were needed. Then with a curt word to "Jewey Dick" to keep a sharp eye above ground, the master-criminal slipped a pistol in his pocket, took a bunch of keys from the safe in the study, provided himself with an electric-torch, and made his way along a series of corridors until he came to the east wing of the mansion.

Since Plummer's occupancy, this part of the manor had not been in use. The old furniture stood just as it had been when he entered into possession, ghostly-looking relics of bygone days which were in stark contrast to the amazing hive of industry that functioned in the great cellars beneath.

Back in the old days, when priests were harried from one end of England to the other, many of the great old houses had built in to them secret hiding-places known as "priests' holes," and it was the discovery of such a retreat as this that had partially influenced Plummer in his purchase of Marsden Manor. Not even Jewey Dick knew the secret of the priests hole in the east wing; all he had received of Plummer's confidence was that there was a means of reaching the inner cellars that lay beneath that part of the house without using the main stairs. Soon after entering into possession, Plummer had had the normal entrance to those cellars blocked up with cement, and then the face of the cement aged so that it might appear to have been done many years before.

It was simply one of those streaks of caution which Plummer exhibited from time to time, for, while he had had created still another means of reaching the cellars from the grounds, he had kept this passage for the use of himself and Vali Mata-Vali in case of urgent need.

In a vast sitting-room that occupied one corner of the wing he stood listening before locking the door after him. Then, apparently satisfied, he walked across to the huge fireplace which was high enough to allow him to step inside by bending his head. At the back of this he pressed a secret spring which enabled him to push back one of the big lining stones, disclosing a black opening about four feet high by three feet wide.

Pushing the torch ahead of him, he bent low and wormed his way through. Now he was standing at the top of a flight of very narrow stone stairs, so narrow indeed that he was forced to turn half-sideways before attempting to descend. On his right was a small wooden door, behind which was the priests' hole, and when he had closed the stone after him, Plummer pushed the door open.

The tiny cell contained a wooden bench, a table and a chair, all of oak and black with age, just as they had been left for hundreds of years. On the bench was an assortment of garments, and on the table a black leather bag, which, had it been opened, would have revealed a very complete assortment of materials for disguise. There was enough here for a quick change for himself and Vali should they be forced to leave "on the run."

Satisfied that no one had tampered with them, Plummer closed the door and started down the stairs. There were exactly twenty-nine, and, at the bottom, a passage no wider than the stairs which ran for a matter of twenty feet or so before ending in another strong oaken door. It was heavily barred and bolted on Plummer's side, but before removing those barriers he stood once more to listen. Through the door came to him a faint, humming sound, so slight that one could not have caught it had not one been seeking it.

It brought a gleam of satisfaction to the eyes of the master-criminal, and now he slid off the iron bar, after which he took out the bunch of keys which he had taken from the safe in the study, selected one, and fitted it to the lock.

When he drew the door open he stepped into a small cellar about twelve feet square. He left the door closed, but unlocked and opened another door which admitted him into a room that revealed an extraordinary scene for such a place. It was a long cellar lined with benches, at which a dozen men were bent over tasks that seemed to engross their keenest attention. Just above the head of each man was a powerful arc-light, and, attached to ceiling-brackets, running the full length of the benches, were bearing shafts, with flexible connections hanging at intervals.

In the ends of these connections were fitted tools which rotated at high speed, and which each workman employed in the task in hand. On the right of each man was, too, a small grinding wheel which could be sent into an amazing number of revolutions per minute by making a connection with another shaft that ran beneath the work benches. On the benches and in front of each man was an array of tools, the use of which would have been recognised readily enough by anyone who had any knowledge of the diamond-cutting industry.

Finally, on a square piece of clean chamois, a little removed from each man's left arm, glittered what, at first, appeared to be bits of glass of many hues, but which were, in fact, precious stones of great value—diamonds, emeralds, sapphires, and rubies. It was, to be exact, a perfectly equipped establishment for the cutting and polishing of precious stones, and had one made sufficiently exhaustive inquiries in that trade on the Continent, one might have discovered that a dozen or so of the cleverest crook cutters known to Amsterdam had not been heard of for some months past. George Marsden Plummer could have answered the riddle of their whereabouts.

As he stepped into the place a man at the end of one of the long benches rose and hastened towards him. He was a little, wizened old man, with spectacles that held lenses of great thickness. Years before he had been known in the legitimate industry as one of the safest and best cutters at a bench, and he it was who had been entrusted with the cutting of many a famous diamond.

But he was one of the few who had "gone wrong," had been unable to resist the pilfering of small chips, and eventually he had drifted into the shady side of the trade where, like all the others in that cellar, Plummer had marked him down and swept him into his net when he had need of him.

"I was getting worried," he said, speaking in French with a strong Belgian accent. "It is more than two days now since you came."

"I was called away, Gustave," responded Plummer. "Is everything all right?"

The old man nodded and drew a sheet of paper from his pocket.

"We shall finish the present lot by to-morrow night. Then I shall want more stones. I have the list here—they were a fine lot to handle. It was a pity to cut down some of them."

And he sighed, for he was a true artist.

"I know how you feel," said Plummer carelessly, "but it can't be helped. Let me have the list—I'll check it up later. I am glad you have pushed things forward, Gustave, for I want to make a shipment almost at once. I can depend on you to see that they are safely packed."

"Of course, master. Am I not well paid and happy?"

"And the others?"

"Quite content; but before long they will need to get into the open air."

"I shall arrange that before many days. We will let up on the work, and I'll give you all a month's holiday on full pay."

"They will be very grateful, master."

"Sleeping quarters and food all right?"

"Everything goes smoothly, master."

"Good. I shall come back this way. Keep them at it."

He walked along the line of benches, pausing beside each man for a word and to examine the work he had finished. With each he cracked a rough jest that put them into a good humour, for Plummer knew how to handle those who worked for him, and did not underestimate the importance of keeping things running smoothly in this, the very heart of the great scheme that was hidden behind the cover of the Marsden Cycle Works.

At the end of the cellar he unlocked another door with one of the keys on his bunch and stepped into still a third cellar, small like the first he had entered. From here he gained a fourth cellar of about the same size as the one where the gem-cutters were at work. An even louder humming noise broke on his ears, and from where he stood he could see half a dozen small presses at work beneath enormous arc-lamps.

Against the walls were more benches at which men sat with copper plates before them and engraving tools in their hands. Six of the cleverest counterfeiters in all Europe made up that number, and in this underground "factory" were being forged notes on half a dozen big banks located as far apart as London, Paris, Berlin, Madrid, Rome, and Vienna. At one table, quite alone, sat a very young man, slick as a girl in appearance, whose delicate fingers were copying the intricate design of a share certificate of a great American railway. It was, in its way, the inner sanctuary of all Plummer's amazing activities, and the sight of it would have brought tears of joy to the eyes of Detective-inspector Thomas of Scotland Yard, or of Thibaud of the Paris Surete.

Plummer made the round here as in the gem-cutting room, pausing for a word with each man and spending several minutes in critical examination of the partially engraved plates, the fresh notes that were coming off the presses, and the water-marked paper that was exactly similar to that used in the genuine notes. It was the most complete forgery plant that had ever been gathered together in one place.

Lastly he visited a small electric furnace in one corner of the cellar, where a heavily goggled man was watching a sizzling, boiling mass of molten metal. Into that crucible had gone gold coins, gold rings, gold chains, gold watch cases and gold ornaments of every variety; it was the place where every risky bit of precious metal was reduced to solid bulk, and every trace of identification absorbed in the neat little ingots that would be formed when the crucible was emptied.

The master-criminal's strange amber eyes were glittering with a fierce light as he finished his tour. All during his long career he had dreamed of such a complete factory as this—a place into which he could bring the spoils gathered by many agents—a place from which he could send out those same spoils changed beyond all chance of recognition; crime and the proceeds organised on a strictly business basis with a fool-proof "blanket" that would insulate it against the keenest police wits. The Marsden Cycle Factory was that blanket.

Slowly he made his way back as he had come, passing through cellar after cellar, and locking the doors carefully behind him. Those men who toiled beneath the ground like moles slept and ate in the same quarters, but periodically they were allowed at night out into the grounds by the secret way which Plummer had had built by Italian workmen after taking over the Manor.

No risk was there that any would betray him, for each man was "wanted" badly, and in no place could he have found such safety as in the cellars beneath that great old house just outside Slough. And Plummer had meant it when he said he would soon give them a month's holiday on full pay, for he was ready now to wind up things for the time being and let the game simmer until the police of half a dozen capitals should be occupied with other matters.

Moreover he was not a little uneasy over the unpleasant surprise that had been awaiting him in the person of Tinker. Not until the lad had blundered into the Manor had Plummer seen the slightest sign that his secret was in danger; until that moment he had been laughing and jeering at the efforts of the police to trace the perpetrators of the many frauds that were being "pulled off" in England and on the Continent.

But he was more than a little puzzled to know how it came that Tinker had been working in the Marsden works under an assumed name. It could only mean that Sexton Blake was suspicious of—something. But of what?

It was this that exercised his mind as he took one last look into the priests' hole, and, passing by way of the secret stone into the fireplace, closed the way and started towards the west wing of the house.

"I'll learn what is behind it to-night," he snarled, "or I'll tear that whelp to pieces."

CHAPTER 11.   Fitting Up the Raid.

SEXTON BLAKE woke and sat up in bed listening.

On the little table near at hand, the luminous face of a night clock showed the hands pointing to a quarter past one. Not a sound broke the stillness of the night, not even the distant rumble of traffic or the vagrant hooting of a motor-horn. Yet something for which he was as yet unable to account had brought him out of sleep with a jerk. What was it?

He switched on the light by the hanging button at the head of the bed and reached for his dressing-gown. Thrusting his feet into a pair of Indian moccasins, he lit a cigarette and made for the door. He switched on the lights as he went along, illuminating his dressing-gown, the bathroom, Tinker's bed-room, the laboratory, the small sitting-room that was seldom used, the dining-room, and, finally, the hall and consulting-room.

He did not bother descending to the basement where Mrs. Bardell slept, for Pedro, he knew, was sleeping down there, and the bloodhound would make short work of any intruder who was foolhardy enough to attempt an entry that way.

There was still a little fire in the consulting-room so, after examining the windows here as he had in each of the other rooms, he dropped into one of the comfortable saddle-bag chairs and set his wits to work.

"What was it?" he asked himself again and again. "Everything seems in order, and it couldn't have been Pedro growling. Just the same, something yanked me wide awake, and if it wasn't something outside then it must have been some mental jolt within me."

His mind went back to the problems he had been engaged upon just before retiring —the strange sequence of frauds, robberies, and even murders that had taken place in different parts of Europe during the past six or seven months; more particularly the affair at the Paris and Calais Bank in the Haymarket, the big banking fraud in Brussels, the jewel robbery in the Rue de la Paix in Paris, and the most recent of all, the death of Etienne Coppot with the colossal crash of the Coppot Bank that had followed.

Then he brought his thoughts to bear on the last puzzle that had engaged him before turning out his bedside light—Tinker, the reports the lad had sent in, and his odd silence during the two days Blake had spent in Paris. From this it was a quick step to the puzzle of the

Marsdon Cycle factory, and as his thoughts dwelt once more on this, the detective uttered a low exclamation; for, out of the mists of dreams, he suddenly snatched the tenuous link he sought.

It was his sub-conscious self that had driven him into wakefulness; into his dreams there had obtruded something that was the result of his own mental activity while he slept—something that his sub-conscious mind had been struggling with while the conscious rested; and as he realised what it was he came to his feet.

"What a dense creature I've been," he muttered, pacing back and forth the length of the consulting-room. "To think such a thing never occurred to me before! If it is so—if it is feasible then it would explain the whole mystery of that bicycle factory and the prices at which the Marsden bicycle is being sold—not at a figure low enough to excite too much suspicion, but one that would ensure it a wide market. Is it possible? Those frames from so many different makers—from Sheffield, from France, from Belgium; and how would they link up? Ah! Sheffield and the murder of the cashier at the steel works with the robbery of some nine thousand pounds wages; Brussels and the fraud on the bank there; Paris and the robbery in the Rue de la Paix; Paris again and the Coppot affair; London and the swindle at the Haymarket branch of the Paris and Calais Bank,

"But, according to Tinker's reports, shipments received at the Marsden works include among those places only Sheffield, Brussels and France. But if this theory of mine is correct, then no such inward shipment would be necessary in the affair of the Paris and Calais Bank, because London is so near Slough! And, in the Coppot affair there would be time yet for such a shipment to be made if it were a blind for the purpose I suspect.

"If I am right, and I don't deny that the theory seems rather strained, then the proof would lie in the imminence of a fresh shipment from France. Far-fetched, perhaps, but George Marsden Plummer is no ordinary criminal. And if I should be right then there is not a moment to be lost, for if Tinker has fallen into his hands the lad will be in deep peril, while Plummer will wipe out all traces with the least possible delay. It's a gamble that will make me a laughing-stock at Scotland Yard if I am wrong; but if I am right it holds the first chance for a long time of laying Plummer by the heels. Shall I chance it?"

Blake tossed away the end of his cigarette and stood rigid in the centre of the room, his eyes fixed on the dying coals. Gradually one picture arose in his mind, dominating everything else—the vision of Tinker, from whom no report had come for the past two days. And Tinker had spotted Plummer.

Suddenly Blake wheeled and made for the desk. On the telephone calendar were several numbers which he used frequently. One of those was the call of the Post Office at Charing Cross, which is open all night for the dispatch of telegrams, and this it was to which he was put through. When he had given his name, there was no difficulty about dictating his message over the wire, and, while he spoke, he jotted down his own words. When he finally rehung the instrument the following was already being laid out for quick dispatch to Emilc Thibaud of the Paris Surete:

"Please endeavour find out urgently any possible particulars of shipments of bicycle frames and parts from any point in France to Marsden Cycle Company of Slough, England. Suggest British and French Chambers of Commerce in Paris may be able to give some assistance, also try ascertain any shipments projected for early future dates if such discovered. Request you have everything held at point of shipment or in customs until further advices between us. Matter utmost urgency.

"SEXTON BLAKE."

Slipping this copy into the "Outward Telegrams" book, Blake again took up the telephone receiver and gave the number of Inspector Thomas' house in Brixton. There was a little delay before the inspector's voice came over the wire, irritation in his tones at having been woke up at such an hour. But when he heard Sexton Blake he was attentive enough.

"Can you get together fifty or sixty men for a raid to-night?" asked Blake, as if he were inviting the other to go for a drive.

"Fifty or sixty men for a raid—what's up, Blake?"

"A job in Buckinghamshire—at Slough, to be exact. You'll have to fix matters with the Bucks police, but there won't be any difficulty there. If we wait for a lot of red tape it will be too late. It's a gamble, Thomas, but if it comes off it will be the biggest thing you will have brought off for many a long day."

"But what is it, Blake? Fifty or sixty men and a raid into Bucks. If anything goes wrong there will be a lot of carpeting at the Yard."

"I can tell you this much over the phone, and I'll tell you the rest later— it has some connection with the affair at the Haymarket branch of the Paris and Calais Bank, and with the Coppot bank crash in Paris, of which you have probably read."

"Yes; is that all?"

"Not by a jugful. And there is a chance of netting our old friend, George Marsden Plummer."

"Good heavens, why didn't you say so before? I'll get on to the Yard and come up West at once."

"I'll meet you at the Yard."

With that Blake hung up the receiver and rose. In exactly twelve minutes he was dressed and ready for what might come. His last care was to make a careful examination of his automatic before thrusting the big weapon into the side-pocket of his coat; he had chosen his heaviest .45 for this job. Then he made his way round to the garage at the back, and after rousing the night man, took the wheel of the Grey Panther. There was no need to test the big Rolls for petrol or oil; she was kept in constant readiness for the road, day or night.

There was a buzz of subdued excitement at the Yard when Blake arrived, and while it had leaked out that the famous detective had something to do with Thomas' orders, nothing definite was known of the purpose of the projected raid. But already a couple of detective-sergeants were preparing the men for the journey, and in the big yard were two fully equipped vans belonging to the Flying Squad, with their personnel giving the last onceover to details.

Blake was talking with one of the detectives attached to this section when Thomas drove in. He took Blake up at once to his room, where he listened to the brief but amazing sequence of events Blake laid before him, and which, despite the isolated and unconnected nature of each, had been linked up by Blake in theory as forming part of the same whole.

"I repeat, it's a gamble, Thomas," he conceded, when he had finished, "and even now you may not feel like taking the chance. But I'm willing to gamble my reputation on a dud, and you can have the kudos if we pull it off. All that interests me is to net Plummer if he is behind the business, and to rescue Tinker if he is in Plummer's hands. You don't need me to tell you what will be the lad's fate if Plummer suspects why he is there."

Thomas looked worried.

"It's a big responsibility, Blake," he said slowly. "I've been through on the 'phone to the Bucks' police—got the chief constable himself at his private house. He is quite agreeable, and says he will start in his car at once for Slough. But I don't know—I don't know! All you have got to go on is a theory, and if we turn up a dud we shall only look foolish. We don't even know that Plummer is there."

"We know he was there," broke in Blake a little irritably. "And I have given you my reasons for thinking he has some connection with the different crimes I have mentioned. Even if I am wrong, all wrong on every point, you still have enough old stuff to arrest Plummer, and with him under lock and key we should have a chance to find out just what is behind that bicycle factory stunt at Slough. I don't think, Thomas, I have ever let you down, and your position at the Yard is quite strong enough for you to make the raid on suspicion alone."

"There have been a good many shake-ups lately," muttered the inspector, "and I'm getting near the retiring age. I don't want to make a fool of myself at this stage of the game."

Sexton Blake rose to his feet.

"Very well," he said coldly, "you must do as you think fit. I tell you again that it is just possible the biggest coup of your career lies before you to-night—two million francs in Brussels, three million francs in jewels from the Rue de la Paix, nine thouand pounds at Sheffield, close to a million and a quarter francs at the bank in the Haymarket, dozens of other swindles, forgeries, robberies and murders throughout Europe, and a ten-million-franc get-away of the Coppot Bank funds in Paris. And you hesitate! Good-night. At least I shall travel to Slough and search for Tinker."

With that Blake turned and made for the door, but before he reached it the inspector was after him, clutching his sleeve, beads of sweat standing on his forehead.

"Hold on, Blake, do hold on! Don't get shirty. You know I have always banked on your advice, and I know what I have owed to you in the past. Maybe I'm getting old, but this is so—so big. Hang it all, man, give me a chance to think!"

"To think? This is no time for thinking; it is time for action, and darned quick action at that, if we are not to be too late."

Thomas passed a hand across his brow; then he stiffened. Blake knew the signs of old, and smiled inwardly, although his face was stern and cold as before.

"All right, you persistent devil. I'll gamble. Sit down and I'll start things humming."

Blake shrugged, and walking back, dropped into the chair from which he had sprung in what seemed so like high dungeon. Thomas got his finger on a button, and from that moment of his decision Blake could not complain of dilatoriness. He revealed a smoothness of control and an efficiency that revealed why he ranked so high at the Yard.

Within twenty minutes two Flying Squad vans were leading the way towards Hammersmith and Chiswick, where they would pick up the Great West Road, which would bring them to Slough. Back of these came the Grey Panther, with Blake at the wheel, Thomas beside him, and two plain-clothes men in the back. Then followed four more plain vans, with two men on driving-seat and a complement of twelve inside each; and, lastly, two more touring cars containing five men to the car, with a third Flying Squad van bringing up the rear.

CHAPTER 12.   Third Degree for Tinker.

WHEN Tinker was jerked into wakefulness by Jimmie he hadn't the faintest idea whether it was night or day. His muscles had become so numbed and his senses so dulled that he was almost oblivious to what passed outside himself. It had seemed hours that he had been lying there since Plummer's first visit, and yet he knew it might only have been a comparatively brief time before the master criminal once more appeared in the cell.

This time there was no preliminary questioning of his gaoler. He spoke a curt word to Jimmie, who untied the bandage about the lad's mouth and dragged out the gag. Next he cut the bonds that secured his arms and legs and heaved him into a sitting posture. But the moment he released his hold Tinker fell back, helpless. Plummer uttered a curse.

"Give him a spot of brandy," he snapped, suiting the action to the word by bringing out his own silver travelling flask. "You've had him tied too tightly—give the blood a chance—rub his-wrists and ankles. He can't talk yet, and he's got to spill some stuff before I finish with him. Get busy."

Jimmie obeyed. He hauled Tinker once more into a sitting position and forced the mouth of the flask between his lips. The fiery spirit burned Tinker's throat, but he was forced to swallow, and a few moments later he felt a warm comforting glow within him. He had neither the will nor the strength to object when Jimmie's big coarse hands began rubbing away at his wrists.

At first, the prickly sensation was almost unbearable; so exquisite was the agony as the blood began to find its way back into the tiny blood vessels from which it had been excluded for so long. But gradually the pain lessened, and he found himself able to move the fingers of one hand, then of the other.

Jimmie applied the same treatment to his ankles while Tinker gently massaged his own jaw. The gag had forced the jawbones so wide and the brutality of the pressure had swollen his tongue to such a thickness that Tinker was quite prepared to swear that he would never articulate clearly again.

But Nature asserted herself as the blood began once more to function without restraint, and by the time Plummer had finished a cigarette Tinker was sufficiently cognisant of what was going on as to cast a speculative eye at him. Whatever had gone before, Tinker knew that he was fast approaching the crisis that had been threatening ever since Plummer discovered his identity. The master criminal meant business and showed it. And Tinker knew enough of Plummer's capacity for evil as well as his capability for inflicting it that he did not make any mistake about what that threatening gaze conveyed.

He guessed fairly correctly that two or three days had passed since he had blundered into Jimmie's arms. He had no idea whether Blake was back in England and, of course, he knew nothing about what had taken Blake to Paris. He had no knowledge of the theory Blake had formed since then; the only connecting link between him and the detective was forged by the few reports he had sent in since his arrival in Slough.

Therefore, he realised his only hope was a very frail thread. If Blake were still in Paris then even that slender thread must snap; if Blake had returned to London then how could he discover what had happened to him (Tinker) before it was too late?

In those few desperate moments while he faced Plummer the lad would have given anything, even his hope of life, to be able to get word to Blake that a big game was being played behind the blanket of the Marsden Cycle works. For he had seen enough now to be sure of that.

He did not move when Plummer pushed Jimmie aside and bent over him.

"That will do, Jimmie. He's all right now. I'll see that he loosens up if he is reluctant." Then he turned his full attention to Tinker. "I'm going to give you a chance," he went on in cold, threatening tones, "a chance, mind you, for one thing —your life. You can take it or leave it; I don't care two straws. But either way you are going to spill what you know. Do you get me?"

Still Tinker did not answer, just stared back defiantly at those amber eyes. Plummer uttered a short ejaculation of anger.

"Dumb already, are you?" he snarled. "I'll loosen your jaw."

With that he made a swift movement and caught hold of Tinker's right wrist. Twisting it backwards he dragged it up between the lad's shoulder blades and kept increasing the pressure until Tinker went white and groaned, despite his determination to give no sign. He made a valiant effort to hammer Plummer's shins with his foot, but Jimmie grabbed them in his great hands and forced them back.

"Feel like talking now?" went on Plummer harshly. "Think you can twist your tongue if you have to? How's that? Nice little sensation, isn't it? Just a fraction of an inch more and the bone will snap at the elbow joint. It's a nasty break that, but not as bad as when the left one snaps, too. And you're going to get more than that, you young whelp. Now—will you talk?"

He gave a last twist that brought the elbow joint so close to the point of being dragged apart that no human could stand up under the agony. Tinker's face was drained of its last atom of blood; his eyes were starting from his head, the sweat was dripping from his forehead and his lower lip was grey where his teeth were gripping it. Another groan came from his throat, and then he went suddenly limp in Plummer's grasp.

"He's off, guv'nor," whispered Jimmie.

The master criminal gave a snort of disgust.

"Shut up, you fool," he said evenly. "Don't you know a dead faint when you see one? Give him another spot of brandy. I guess he'll decide to talk when he comes round."

He released his hold and stood back, lighting another cigarette. Jimmie applied himself to an attempt to resuscitate Tinker, his efforts consisting of pouring a large quantity of brandy down the lad's throat and massaging the neck muscles to force him to swallow. At the end of five minutes or so Tinker came round, held in Jimmie's huge arms while he stared groggily at Plummer.

The master criminal gave him another minute; then he prodded him with his foot.

"Going to talk now?" he asked curtly.

"Wh—what do you wanna know?" stammered Tinker in a hoarse whisper.

"Ah! So it has worked, has it? I thought I'd get a little sense into you. I want you to answer a few simple questions. If you do so, I will keep my word and you shall live. You'll be kept here for the present until I am ready to let you go. But you'll go with a whole skin. If you refuse then you'll go into a nice little electric crucible I have, and you know what that means. You'll be nothing but ashes in an hour, and Sexton Blake can whistle to the Thames for you. Complete annihilation—just that. Got me?"

Tinker nodded weakly.

"I understand," he whispered. "What do you wanna know?"

"Why did you take a job in my factory under an assumed name?"

Tinker was now not so groggy as he appeared. He was playing for time, and he knew that Plummer, in his anxiety to learn what he could, was not likely to go to extreme measures until he knew it was hopeless to get anything out of him without torture. He was weighing in his mind just how much he could say without jeopardising matters for Blake and yet gain for himself every precious minute possible.

"What d'you mean?" he countered after a pause, speaking just when Plummer was showing signs of sharp impatience.

"You know well enough what I mean, so don't stall. I'll give you just so much rope and you can hang yourself if you wish. Answer my question—what were you doing in my factory as 'Charles Turner'? I've seen your works' card, so don't deny it."

"I'm not denying it. I was just there."

"You were sent there by Sexton Blake?"

"Yes."

"What did Blake want to find out? What was his game? Why did he want to get a line on me?"

"He didn't."

"What the deuce do you mean? Cut the lies or I'll finish the job now."

"I'm telling you the truth. The guv'nor didn't know you had any connection with the bicycle factory when he sent to me Slough."

Something in Tinker's tones must have impressed Plummer, for he bent forward and knit his brows in a puzzled way.

"Explain what you're driving at. If he didn't know about me, why did you wangle the job?"

"It was the Marsden bicycle he wanted me to investigate; he didn't know you had anything to do with the machine."

"Then why was he interested?"

"If I tell you I'll be giving away the confidence of one of the guv'nor's clients."

Plummer's lips came back over his teeth in a snarl. Like a flash his hand shot out and gripped Tinker's wrist. Once more he jammed the right arm high up between the shoulder-blades.

"You young whelp, I'll smash it this time if you don't spit what you know darned quick. Are you going to talk?"

Tinker uttered a suppressed scream that sounded genuine enough as an expression of terror. Nor was it difficult to put an agonised timbre into his tones, for the pain was excruciating. Yet he stood it as long as he could, for he was still playing for time.

"I'll talk," he gasped.

Plummer released his arm and stood back.

"That's the last time I use those means," he said evenly. "So you'd better hurry up."

"If—if I tell you why I came to the factory will you let me go?" asked Tinker, in pleading tones.

"You'll save your skin—that's all the terms I'll make. Now spit it out."

Tinker saw that he dared not strain the point farther, so, as if coming to a sudden decision, he looked up.

"I told you it was the Marsden bicycle."

"Why?"

"A Mr. Mendley came to the guv'nor, and asked him to try and find out why the Marsden bicycle could be sold at so much less than the Mendley machine. He said the parts were of the same standard, and that the Marsden could not be sold at the price and show a profit. He was worried because he couldn't afford to reduce the price of his bicycle. He had put his own men into the Marsden factory at different times, but they had found nothing. He thought there must be some monkeying with the quality going on, and asked the guv'nor to try and find out where it was. I know something about that sort of thing, so the guv'nor sent me out to get a job. That's all."

Plummer showed nothing of the vast relief that suddenly swept through him, for he felt that Tinker was telling the truth.

"Do you swear that?"

"Yes."

"That is the only reason you came to Slough?"

"Yes—honest."

The master criminal laughed suddenly. Then his eyes grew wary.

"And did you find anything?"

"You know I didn't. I thought there must be something when I recognised you as the head of the works, and knew how the bicycle had got its name. But I saw the thing was on the level."

"Then why did you try to break in here?"

"Because I thought I might find out the secret. Mr. Mendley said you must be selling the Marsden bicycle almost at a loss."

"Have you made any report to Sexton Blake?

"Y-yes."

"Did you tell him you had seen me?"

"Y-yes."

"Ah! So he knows that, oh? That puts a different complexion on it. I don't know just how far you are trying to spoof me you young ape, but I'm taking no chances on you. Keep him safe in here, Jimmie; I'll decide by the morning what to do with him."

"But you promised—" began Tinker.

"Shut up," snarled Plummer. "I haven't half finished with you."

He turned towards the door, but before he reached it there was a sharp knocking, and it opened to reveal Jewey Dick in a state of palpable excitement.

"Come quickly, guv'nor!" he whispered hoarsely. "There's the devil and all to pay!"

CHAPTER 13.　The Flying Squad.

FEW, if any, persons suspected the meaning of that procession of cars that swept along the Great Western Road that night.

The vans were too well camouflaged for any casual observer to guess what they contained, and the men in the open cars might have been any ordinary party of citizens who had been kept late in town by some lodge dinner.

At Slough there was a halt while Inspector Thomas and Blake entered the police station in search of the local inspector. The chief constable had promised to get through to him and advise him what to expect, so they found the other waiting, puzzled, and, at first, a little inclined to be cool.

"Mr. Marsden, of the Marsden Cycle Works," he said, in answer to Thomas' question. "Certainly I know where he lives. He has Marsden Manor, about two miles out of the town."

"On the main road?"

"Yes. But what is wrong? Mr. Marsden hasn't been here long, but he is very popular with his workpeople and the townsfolk, As a matter of fact, he has been away for the last few days, but got back this evening, so I am informed by one of the constables; his man met him at Victoria."

"Then he must have travelled Newhaven —Dieppe," thought Blake, who, so far, was taking no part in the conversation.

"I have no doubt that Mr. Marsden has made a good impression locally," rejoined Thomas quietly, "nevertheless we have urgent business with him. You have heard from the chief constable that I am to have a free hand?"

"Yes."

"I shall be glad if you will join us, but we have no time to lose. I was hoping that Major Barrington would be here by now."

"He ought to turn up at any moment. I shall certainly join you, for it is my district and my duty. But I think I should be told what is wrong."

Thomas glanced swiftly at Blake; the latter gave a slight nod.

"Ever hear of ex-inspector George Marsden Plummer, of Scotland Yard?" asked Thomas curtly.

The local man nodded. Everyone in every police force of England knew of the blot that was cast upon one of the finest bodies of men in the world when Plummer, an inspector at the Yard, fell from grace and turned to criminal ways.

"Well," went on Thomas, "your Mr. Marsden, of the Marsden Cycle Works, is George Marsden Plummer. He hasn't taken the trouble to invent a new name. That is why we are here."

The local man's eyes opened wide. He gave Thomas a searching look; then glanced at Sexton Blake. Something in the grim set of the latter's jaw must have told him Thomas was not romancing. And now he began to realise just why Scotland Yard had thought it worth while to send their senior inspector out to Slough at that hour of fhe night.

"How many men shall I get together?" he asked, after a pause. "I didn't dream of anything like this."

"Don't worry about men," cut in Thomas. "I've got more than fifty outside. All I want is to be shown the way to this Manor. I'll take care of the rest. And as the chief constable hasn't turned up yet, we'll have to go without him."

Scarcely had he finished speaking, however, when the door opened and a tall, military-looking man entered with brisk step. He nodded to the local inspector, and then, as his eyes fell on Blake, his face lit up with a charming smile.

"Why, Blake, you are in on this, are you? I'm glad to sec you. 'Evening, Inspector Thomas. Just what is up?"

Blake shook hands, for he and Major Barrington were old friends, having met first in South India, where Barrington was District Commissioner of Indian Police. Thomas made a gesture towards Blake.

"Better tell the chief constable, Blake. I'll fix up things with Inspector Malling."

Blake and Major Barrington walked aside, and, as briefly as possible, Blake explained the meaning of the summons at such an hour of the night; when he finished the other gave a low whistle.

"George Marsden Plummer, eh? And at the Manor! My dear fellow, are you sure? You amaze me. This 'Mr. Marsden' who has put up the cycle works here seems to be one of the most popular men in the district."

"He is none other than George Marsden Plummer nevertheless," returned Blake. "I have too much confidence in my young assistant to fear that he would make a mistake."

"Then let us get him without delay."

Thomas rejoined them just then, and when Blake had made

private arrangements with the local station for a constable to be sent to the boarding establishment where Tinker had put up. Blake followed the others out to where the string of cars was waiting.

It was a quick run out to Marsden Manor. Inspector Malling had given Thomas a clear idea of the lay of the land, and had described how the grounds were surrounded by a high, spike-protected wall. Major Barrington, who knew the place well, did a like service for Blake, so before they reached the place the four were able to form a plan of campaign.

This consisted simply of keeping the main fleet of cars back and allowing only Blake's Grey Panther to proceed as far as the main front gates. Blake, Thomas, and the two men from the Yard were to get out and wait a little distance away in the shadow of the wall while Inspector Malling and Major Barrington rang the bell.

If their summons was answered, then it was their job to keep the gate open until Blake and his companions should come up. The rest of the force was to be strung round the surrounding wall with all three Flying Squad vans in position in front of the main gates. It looked, like a watertight plan that could not misfire.

Up to the moment of the wooden door in the larger gate being opened, everything went according to plan. But just here a hitch occurred which no one could have foreseen. It was "Jewey Dick" who, in Plummer's absence in the cellars, took it upon himself to see who was ringing at that hour of the night.

He knew perfectly well from Plummer that the latter stood all right with the local inspector and the police; but Jewey Dick had never had enough interest in the matter to inquire the name of the inspector. Nor had he ever set eyes on him, for the simple reason that he had stuck close to the Manor ever since his arrival.

But years before when Inspector Malling was a sergeant in the Henley district, Jewey Dick had run foul of him over a somewhat serious lapse in judgment, with the result that, on Sergeant Malling's evidence, he had done a "stretch."

Just before opening the gate, Jewey Dick had turned on an electric bulb which Plummer had had fixed above the gate so that the one opening the wicket at night would be able to see the features of the visitor. On this occasion the downflare revealed not only Malling's face to Jewey Dick, but the latter's smug countenance to the inspector. The result was entirely mutual—one of dumbfounded surprise; but if

Inspector Malling had entertained any doubts as to the wisdom of a night raid on Marsden Manor, they vanished at sight of the old lag.

Jewey Dick was the first to break the spell. He made one frantic effort to slam the door, but Major Barrington, who had sensed something out of the ordinary, hurled himself against it. Jewey Dick did not wait for any more.

Turning, he sped as fast as his legs would carry him through the heavily-timbered park towards the mansion. And it was just because of his superior knowledge of the layout of the grounds that he reached the front entrance a good half minute in advance of his leading pursuers.

It was some moments before Blake and his companions were through the gate in pursuit of Malling and Major Barrington, but what they lost in delay they made up in speed, so that by the time Major Barrington was violently ringing the bell of the Grange they reached the porch.

"What happened?" asked Thomas, panting heavily.

Malling explained.

"What about smashing in the door, major?" went on Thomas. "It's Plummer, and it looks as if Blake was right. He'll give us the slip yet if we don't watch out!"

"We'll get him!" jerked the chief constable. "The place is surrounded; he can't get away. What do you think, Blake?"

"I am inclined to agree with Inspector Thomas. I've seen Plummer wriggle out of as tight a corner as this."

"All right. I'll give one more ring, and if that isn't answered we'll smash a way in."

He jammed his finger on the button, and, somewhere inside, they could hear the shrilling of the bell; and, at that same moment, Jewey Dick was hammering at the door of the small cellar where Plummer was striving to torture information out of Tinker.

It needed only a few words for Plummer to grasp that something very serious was threatening. He had taken care to cultivate a nodding acquaintance with the local inspector, and, under ordinary circumstances, would have had no fear of Malling visiting him at the Grange.

But when Jewey Dick spoke of another man with him, and blurted out that Malling had recognised him, Plummer knew the ice was very thin. Besides, there was the lateness of the hour and the fact that Jewey Dick had so far lost his nerve as to turn tail and run.

Plummer shifted a threatening eye to Jimmie.

"You stick here and keep your eye on that whelp," he snarled. "You, Jewey, get going. I'll settle this business upstairs."

He tore through the cellars at top speed and gained the first floor. The moment he stepped into the main hall, however, he knew that no bluff would serve this crisis, for heavy blows were being delivered on the thick oaken door, and Plummer had been cornered too often not to know the meaning of that sound.

Something had gone wrong, radically wrong, and swiftly his mind flew to Tinker and Sexton Blake. He flung a few words over his shoulder at Jewey Dick as he ran towards a small cloak-room that was on the right of the front door.

"Upstairs with you and call mademoiselle and Anna," he snapped. "Get them down here as quick as you can. I'll see to the door."

Jewey Dick took the stairs two at a time, while Plummer jerked open the door of the cloak-room and reached for one of the switches on a small wall board. Pressing it down, he slid aside a square panel which allowed him to look out through a peephole and scrutinise anyone who stood on the porch for the switch had illuminated a powerful bulb above the door.

The sudden glare had arrested the assault on the oak, and at the moment when Plummer peered out six men stood immobile. With narrowing eye he counted them, and cursed softly as he recognised Malling, Inspector Thomas, and Sexton Blake. Major Barrington he did not know, nor did he recognise the two plain-clothes men, but the latter were stamped only too plainly for what they were.

His fingers itched to drag out his pistol and shoot them down as they stood, Sexton Blake above all, for he knew well enough now that whatever had brought Tinker to Slough it was some suspicion of the secret that lay behind the bicycle works that had inspired Blake to initiate this raid. Nor was Plummer fool enough to think that the six men on the porch represented the full complement.

As a matter of fact, it was the turning on of the light that had caused them to desist, thinking that, at last, someone was coming to answer the summons. But Sexton Blake guessed something of the truth, and, drawing back, made a rush at the oak. As his body crashed against it, Plummer jerked up the switch, and, turning, dashed out into the hall.

He knew that the door could not long withstand the combined assault of the six heavy-weights on the porch, and there was precious little time to do what he had to do before making his escape.

At that moment he caught sight of Vali Mata-Vali coming down the stairs. Behind her were Jewey Dick and Anna, the maid. Plummer motioned imperatively, and paused half-way down the hall to press a button that had been fixed to the wall.

No sound could be heard here, but below in the cellar where Jimmie watched over Tinker, and in the great, hidden inner cellars where the gem cutters and forgers were at work, half a dozen big alarm gongs were ringing madly. It was the signal that would be understood, and each one who heard it knew that now it was every man for himself.

Plummer grabbed Vali Mata-Vali by the arm and dashed to the end of the hall. The crashes on the big oaken door were louder than ever, and he hesitated by the door of the study as a terrific rending of wood caught his ear. He abandoned whatever idea he had of entering the room, and kicked open the door into the corridor leading to the eastern wing. He carried Vali along with him, while Jewey Dick dragged Anna at his heels.

It was the first time that any of Plummer's three companions had seen the secret stone at the back of the fireplace in the great salon. Vali paid little attention, for Plummer had already told her about it, but Jewey Dick noted the position of the secret spring carefully, thinking the knowledge might come in useful at a future date. But Fate was turning the wheel so that it would be many a long day before Jewey Dick would find any interest beyond the walls of Broadmoor Prison.

As soon as the stone swung open Plummer pushed Vali and Anna into the monk's cell. Jewey Dick would have followed, but the master criminal caught him by the arm.

"You come with me!" he snapped.

Down the narrow stairs he dashed for the second time that night. At the bottom he unlocked and flung open the door, motioning for Jewey Dick to follow him. Then on through the intervening cellars until he reached the gem-cutting room. At this last door he pushed Jewey against the wall.

"Get your gun out and stand here," he ordered. "That mob will be in the house by now. No telling how soon they will get down here. You hold this door until I get back—I'll not be more than a few moments. If you aren't here when I return I'll take your skin off in little pieces."

Plummer wheeled, and, dragging out his automatic, went plunging down the room where all was confusion. The gem-cutters were crowded at one end, where a few of them had already managed to crawl through a hole that gave into a sloping chute which led to the grounds above.

It was the secret means of exit which Plummer had built against just such a crisis at this. The wizened little foreman, game to the last, was standing by urging his men through before following. In one hand he clutched a big, chamois leather bag, at sight of which Plummer's amber eyes glinted.

"Good man!" he snapped. "Keep them on the move. It's everyone for himself; the flatties are inside and outside. Make for the back gate and then separate. If you reach London you know where to hang out until I come; if you can make Paris, do so; I'll find you at the usual place. Give me the bag!"

Obediently the other handed it over, and, leaving him to it, Plummer went dashing on until he reached the far cellar where the forgeries had been under production. The men here seemed to have acted more promptly, for there was only one man to be seen when Plummer appeared.

He was hurling bundles of printed notes and water-marked paper into the crucible over the electric furnace where the molten gold had been sizzling on Plummer's previous visit. Just as the master-criminal reached him he snatched at a pile of copper plates and hurled them after the other items.

"Is that the lot?" asked Plummer, sweeping the place with his gaze.

"Ja!" came the reply in Dutch. "I fix everyding before I was gone."

Plummer made a grab at the last pile of plates and dumped them after the others.

"You come with me, Oscar!" he snapped. "You are too good a man to lose. They can find the presses, and they can have the metal, but they won't strike anything else. Come on—they'll be tearing the house to pieces in a few minutes!"

Catching the Dutch forger by the shoulder, he turned him round and started him on the run for the door. He carried him right through with him until he reached the inner door of the gem-cutting cellar, where Jewey Dick still stood on guard. The last of the gem-cutters had disappeared.

"Hear anything?"

Jewey shook his head at the question.

"Sounds up above, but nothing close. The gang has beat it."

"I know. Come on, Oscar, up the stairs with you. You go next, Jewey. I'll lock the door and follow."

Thus they gained the monk's cell where Vali Mata-Vali and Anna were sitting on the wooden bench waiting. Plummer pushed Jewey and Oscar to one side and flung the disguises to the floor. He picked out a long cloak for Vali and a hat; then he passed her the chamois bag that was stuffed with the jewels that had been hastily snatched from the cutting benches. Next he dragged the bench aside, and, leaning down. lifted a trapdoor that lay flush with the floor. Another flight of steps was disclosed.

"Down with you, Jewey. You next, Vali. Then you go, Anna, and you follow, Oscar. I have something to do. You will find a passage at the bottom, Vali. Follow it until you come to a door. It isn't locked. Wait there not more than five minutes for me. If I don't come by that time keep right on until you reach some steps. They will bring you to the ground in an old shed across the road and outside the wall. Take the car you will find there and clear out for London. The car is ready for the road. Now go."

Vali Mata-Vali shook her head.

"But what of you? What have you to do?"

Plummer pushed Jewey Dick towards the hole and urged Vali to follow.

"Don't you worry about me. I'm going to try and get a shot at that swab, Sexton Blake. I'll come all right. Now beat it, Jewey."

He was out of the monks' hole and passing through into the fireplace before Vali could stop him. He did not allow the pivotal stone to close fully, but left it ajar an inch or so. Then, with his weapon in his hand, Plummer made for the door, which he unlocked and threw open.

Standing in the corridor outside he could hear sounds in another part of the house, and knew that the police were prosecuting a vigorous search. His teeth drew back in one of his characteristic snarls, and he crept cautiously along the passage leading to the west wing. As he progressed the sounds reached him more and more plainly, and then, suddenly, as he opened a door and peered into the hall, he heard a voice that he knew to be Sexton Blake's, and none other.

"Nothing up there, Thomas," Blake was saying. "But the rooms have been occupied very recently. Barrington may have found something in the study. But Plummer must be near at hand. With the walls surrounded they can't escape us now. I'm going to try the cellars. Will you come with me? I'm going to find Plummer, if I have to take this house apart."

Next moment there was a thud as Blake landed on the floor from the stairs and swung round the big newel post. He was half-way down the hall when Plummer stepped out.

"Going to find me, are you?" he cried tantalisingly. "Well, here I am. Take that, you dirty 'tec!"

He pulled the trigger, and a bullet whizzed past Blake's ear. The detective flung up his own .45 and began shooting as he ran. The master-criminal fired rapidly, literally spraying the air about Blake's head and body with lead. Inspector Thomas came along behind Blake, but now was dashing towards a big oaken seat behind which he dropped and began to shoot. The spitting of the pistols brought Major Barrington and two men out of the study, and, after one startled exclamation, the Chief Constable took a hand in the game.

It was the last shot in Blake's weapon that took first effect. As the pistol crashed out for that last time he saw Plummer reel and fling back against the half-open door. At the same moment Blake felt something sear his right arm, paralysing the nerves and muscles, and causing his weapon to fall to the floor. Again Plummer pulled the trigger, but only a dead "click" followed, and, with a harsh laugh, he disappeared, slamming the door after him.

"Quick!" gasped Blake, who was still staggering about. "Don't let him give us the slip now!"

Despite his wound, he was the first to reach the door, but it needed the other four to smash it open, for Plummer had turned the key on the other side. And it was Major Barrington's electric torch that picked up the blood trail that led them through passage after passage straight to the drawing-room in the east wing, and then to the great fireplace where a little pool of blood on the fireplace showed where the fleeing criminal must have paused.

Blake pushed his way in beside Major Barrington, who was examining the stone.

"I've had some experience of these old secret passages, major; let me see what I can do."

The Chief Constable stood to one side and held the torch close to the stone, for, although one of the plain-clothes men had switched on the electric lights, the big mantle cast a shadow inside the fireplace. But as Blake bent forward the other's eyes widened at the sight of a slow drip, drip, drip that fell from Blake's wrist and splashed on the stone beside the patch which Plummer had left behind him.

"Hang it, man, you, are wounded!" he burst out, moving over quickly. "Come away and have it attended to. I'll find the spring."

But Blake shook his head grimly.

"It isn't much, and I'm sticking to this until I get hold of Plummer. Plenty of time afterwards. Ah!"

He uttered the exclamation as his exploring fingers touched the spring he was seeking. The stone moved a tiny bit, and, at his pressure, swung wide. Major Barrington thrust the torchlight into the opening and gave vent to an epithet as he caught sight of the narrow stairs and the oaken door of the monks' hole. Blake was already through, and the others pressed after him.

They examined the cell first, little guessing that here was the way they should follow if they were to lay their quarry by the heels. But at sight of its emptiness they poured down the stairs, Blake in the lead, for he had another care in his mind— the finding of Tinker. The vicious daring with which Plummer had invaded the hall and started shooting had filled him with an increased uneasiness over the lad.

They were brought up shaply by the barred and bolted door that gave access to the hidden cellars, and it took a full quarter of an hour before they were able to smash it in. A further delay occurred at the second door, but it was obvious to all by now, that they were on a hot scent, and the moment Blake, Major Barrington, and Inspector Thomas stepped into the gem-cutting room they began to realise what an amazing and important discovery they had made.

Their investigations were interrupted at this point, however, by the return of one of the plain-clothes men who had gone above to see how things were progressing.

"Nearly twenty of them captured in the grounds, sir," he said to Major Barrington. "They seemed to come from a hole that was camouflaged by a tree, and were making for the back gate. The guards outside report that none have passed over the walls or through the gates, so it looks as if we have them all, sir,"

The chief constable returned to Blake.

"Better come up and look them over, Blake. Maybe Plummer is among them."

Blake started to shake his head obstinately, but suddenly he staggered a little, and smiled a little crookedly as Thomas shot out a brawny arm to support him.

"I think I will," he said shakily. "This thing has got me more than I thought. Will you have the cellars searched thoroughly, major? I'm very anxious about Tinker."

"You leave the rest to me, old man. You've put the biggest thing in the way of the police that has happened for a long time, or I miss my guess."

Blake would not hear of the chief constable or Thomas coming with him. He accepted the arm of a plain-clothes man, and made his way back slowly to the upper floor, and then along to the west wing. He arrived in the study just in time to hear a further batch of men from the grounds bringing in their prisoners and, a few moments later, three more appeared with Jimmie between them, and Tinker limping slowly along beside them. Needless to say, Blake and the lad did not display their feelings before the others, but Blake gave no thought to his own wound when he saw the haggard expression that still lay in the lad's eyes.

"You've been through it, young 'un," he said in a low tone. "Was it pretty bad?"

"Nothing to worry about, guv'nor, but it looked like being a nasty passage just before you turned up. Have you got Plummer?"

"Not yet, but I hope—"

He was interrupted by the entry of Major Barrington and Inspector Thomas, who had lined up the prisoners in the hall. They reported the further discovery of the printing machinery and electric furnace in still another inner cellar, and Thomas' eyes were glittering with the light of a great triumph.

"The biggest thing in years, Blake," he said in a low tone. "I'll never forget what you've done in this. We've bagged a score of the cleverest crooks in Europe. There isn't a man who hasn't been wanted for ages. And we've struck the swellest counterfeiting plant that has come to light in all my years of service. This thing is going to make Europe sit up."

"But what about Plummer?"

"Nary a sign yet, but I'm hoping we'll find him stuck away in some hiding place."

His hope was doomed not to be realised, however, for while they were going over the prisoners one of the Flying Squad men rushed in to announce that a big touring car had dashed out suddenly from what had seemed to be a deserted and dilapidated shed that stood on a piece of open ground almost opposite the front gates of Marsden Manor.

A police van was off in pursuit, and an examination of the interior of the shed had revealed it to be a cleverly camouflaged garage fitted for every emergency. Blake needed no more than that to suspect the truth; and when he learned that there were at least four persons in the car he guessed that Vali Mata-Vali was one of them.

• •   •   •   •

Thomas was not wrong in predicting a sensation when the Press got hold of the facts. It brought the reporters pouring into Slough, and every detail of the hidden cellars of Marsden Manor was shown in photographs which were scanned by an eager public. Before the search was over a large packet of uncut gems was found in the safe in the study, and these were later identified by the jeweller in the Rue de la Paix as part of the stock that had been taken from his establishment. But that was all the haul.

It was only when Sexton Blake made certain suggestions to Inspector Thomas that the full range of Plummer's cunning became known, and it was through Major Barrington that the elated reporters at last got the truth of the secret that lay behind the Marsden Cycle works at Slough. Nothing would do but that Blake's house in Baker street must be besieged until the detective consented to make a statement.

"It was obvious," he said to a select few who were admitted to the consulting-room as a delegation, "that the notorious criminal, Plummer, and his partner, known as Vali Mata-Vali, must have organised a very exceptional criminal service. When Peter J, Mendley came to me to make certain commercial investigations on his behalf I sent my assistant, Tinker, out to Slough to find a job in the Marsden

Cycle works. I little dreamed then that George Marsden Plummer was the head of the business, but when Tinker reported to me that this was so I began to wonder why he was engaged in the apparently prosaic and honest occupation of manufacturing bicycles. Then other matters came to my attention which gave me a link here and another there— little arrows, so to speak, were discovered that pointed at Plummer."

Then Blake gave them a resume of the theory he had built up around the various frauds, swindles, burglaries, and murders that had been puzzling the police for so long, winding up with the Coppot affair.

"It was obvious that Plummer's greatest problem would be to get rid of the loot," he went on. "Well, one thing that struck me was the portability of everything that figured in the different crimes—precious gems, paper money, both genuine and counterfeit, and such side lines as forged letters of credit. Gold, of course, was different, but melted down to bullion it could be negotiated easily enough. The gems were more risky, but you have seen how he established the gem cutting plant in the cellars of the Manor. But just cast your mind to those things I have mentioned, and tell me if each and all of them could be secreted in the hollow frames of bicycles?"

The listeners nodded breathlessly.

"There is little more. The loot was received at the factory at Slough secreted in the frames as I have suggested, and that is why they were bought at points so diverse and far apart as Sheffield, Brussels, and towns in France. Per contra, the re-cut stones were sealed in small tubes and shipped away to various places abroad by the same means; in this manner, too, the counterfeit notes and forged letters of credit were rolled up and smuggled away. That is all, gentlemen, except one thing."

"What is that, Mr. Blake?"

The pencils paused and were poised expectantly, while the eager eyes of the reporters bombarded the detective. Blake took up a telegram from his desk.

"When this solution of the mystery occurred to me I sent a telegram to Monsieur Emile Thibaud, of the Paris Surete, asking him to ascertain if any shipments of bicycle frames were on the point of being made to the Marsden Cycle Co. from any place in France. He telegraphed me yesterday to the effect that a consignment of five thousand francs had been intercepted at Havre, which were being sent via Southampton.

"I telegraphed further, suggesting that he should have a thorough search made of the frames. His reply will interest you. It runs: 'After probing frames as suggested, have discovered nearly ten million francs currency notes, serial numbers of which correspond to many known to have been acquired at different times by Etienne Coppot. There can be no doubt that whole sum was embezzled by Coppot from bank, and taken from him after he was murdered. Accept warmest congratulations. Am informed by auditor that Coppot Bank will pay depositors in full.'"

Blake laid the paper down and rose.

"Now, gentlemen, if you will excuse me—"

"But Plummer, Mr. Blake, and the beautiful Vali Mata-Vali—what of them?"

Blake shook his head.

"That is a question I cannot answer at present. They escaped on the night we raided the Manor. But you may rest assured that the day will come when they will be forced once more into the open. It would take more than the ten millions from Coppot's bank, which he hoped to made sceure to keep George Marsden Plummer out of crime."

"Then you think he murdered Coppot?"

Blake shrugged

"Quien sabe, as the Spaniards say. Who knows? Good-night, gentlemen."

And, seeing there was no more to come, the excited reporters thanked him and dashed out to the street.

THE END.
[45000 WORDS]

Printed in Great Britain
by Amazon

19509738R00068